Also by Monique Roffey

FICTION

sun dog

The White Woman on the Green Bicycle

Archipelago

House of Ashes

The Tryst

NONFICTION

With the Kisses of His Mouth

The
Mermaid
of
Black Conch

The
Mermaid
of
Black Conch

Monique Roffey

 Alfred A. Knopf · New York · 2022

THIS IS A BORZOI BOOK
PUBLISHED BY ALFRED A. KNOPF

All rights reserved. Published in the United States by
Alfred A. Knopf, a division of Penguin Random House LLC,
New York, and distributed in Canada by Penguin Random House
Canada Limited, Toronto. Originally published in Great Britain by
Peepal Tree Press, Leeds, in 2020.

www.aaknopf.com

Knopf, Borzoi Books, and the colophon are registered trademarks of
Penguin Random House LLC.

Library of Congress Cataloging-in-Publication Data
Names: Roffey, Monique, author.
Title: The mermaid of Black Conch / Monique Roffey.
Description: First American Edition | New York : Alfred A. Knopf,
[2020]
Identifiers: LCCN 2021032416 (print) |
LCCN 2021032417 (ebook) | ISBN 9780593534205 (hardcover) |
ISBN 9780593534212 (ebook)
Classification: LCC PR6118.O37 M47 2020b (print) |
LCC PR6118.O37 (ebook) | DDC 823.92—dc23
LC record available at https://lccn.loc.gov/2021032416
LC ebook record available at https://lccn.loc.gov/2021032417

Jacket illustration by Sophie Bass
Jacket design by Jenny Carrow

Manufactured in the United States of America
First American Edition

For Irma, Laure, and Yvette, and those ancestren before them, for those womxn I'm born from. Pisa, Port Said, Port of Spain. For the Goddess, the muse, the legends of the deep you are, to me.

On the previous day [8 January 1493], when the Admiral went to the Rio del Oro [on Haiti], he said he quite distinctly saw three mermaids, which rose well out of the sea; but they are not so beautiful as they are said to be, for their faces had some masculine traits. The Admiral says that he had seen some, at other times, on the coast of Guinea, where you find manequeta.

A stranger to tears, she did not weep.
A stranger to clothes, she did not dress.
They pocked her with cigarette ends and with burnt
    corks,
And rolled on the tavern floor in raucous laughter.

Pablo Neruda,
"Fable of the Mermaid and the Drunks"

The
Mermaid
of
Black Conch

1

Simplicity

≈≈≈

DAVID BAPTISTE'S DREADS ARE GREY and his body wizened to twigs of hard black coral, but there are still a few people around St. Constance who remember him as a young man and his part in the events of 1976, when those white men from Florida came to fish for marlin and instead pulled a mermaid out of the sea. It happened in April, after the leatherbacks had started to migrate. Some said she arrived with them. Others said they'd seen her before, those who'd fished far out. But most people agreed that she would never have been caught at all if the two of them hadn't been carrying on some kind of flirty-flirty behaviour.

Black Conch waters nice first thing in the morning. David Baptiste often went out as early as possible, trying to beat the other fishermen to a good catch of king fish or red snapper. He would head to the jagged rocks one mile or so off Murder Bay, taking with him his usual accoutrements to keep him company while he put his lines out—a stick of the finest local ganja and his guitar, which he didn't play too well, an old beat-up thing his cousin, Nicer Country, had given him. He would drop anchor near those rocks, lash the rudder, light his spliff and strum to himself while the white, neon disc of the sun appeared on the horizon, pushing itself up, rising slow slow, omnipotent into the silver-blue sky.

David was strumming his guitar and singing to himself when she first raised her barnacled, seaweed-clotted head from the flat, grey sea, its stark hues of turquoise not yet stirred. Plain so, the mermaid popped up and watched him for some time before he glanced around and caught sight of her.

"Holy Mother of Holy God on earth," he exclaimed. She ducked back under the sea. Quick quick, he put down his guitar and peered hard. It wasn't full daylight yet. He rubbed his eyes, as if to make them see better.

"Ayyy," he called across the water. "Dou dou. Come. Mami wata! Come. Come, nuh."

He put one hand on his heart because it was leaping around inside his chest. His stomach trembled with desire and fear and wonder because he knew what he'd seen. A woman. Right there, in the water. A red-skinned woman, not black, not African. Not yellow, not a Chinee woman, or a woman with golden hair from Amsterdam. Not a blue woman, either, blue like a damn fish. Red. She was a red woman, like an Amerindian. Or anyway, her top half was red. He had seen her shoulders, her head, her breasts, and her long black hair like ropes, all sea mossy and jook up with anemone and conch shell. A merwoman. He stared at the spot of her appearance for some time. He took a good look at his spliff; was it something real strong he smoke that morning? He shook himself and gazed hard at the sea, waiting for her to pop back up.

"Come back," he shouted into the deep greyness. The mermaid had held her head up high above the waves, and he'd seen a certain expression on her face, like she'd been studying him.

He waited.

But nothing happened. Not that day. He sat down in his pirogue and, for some reason, tears fell for his mother, just like that. For Lavinia Baptiste, his good mother, the bread baker of the village, dead not two years. Later, when he racked his brain, he thought of all those stories he'd heard since childhood, tales of half-and-half sea creatures, except those stories were of mermen. Black Conch legend told of mermen who lived deep in the sea and came onto land now and then to mate with river maidens—old-time stories, from the colonial era. The older fishermen liked to talk in Ce-Ce's parlour on the foreshore, sometimes late into the night, after many rums and too much marijuana. The mermen of Black Conch were just that: stories.

It was April, time of the leatherback migration south to Black Conch waters, time of dry season, of pouis trees exploding in the hills, yellow and pink, like bombs of sulphur, the time when the whoreish flamboyant begins to bloom. From that moment, when that red-skinned woman rose and disappeared as if to tease him, David ached to see her again. He felt a bittersweet melancholy, a soft caress to his spirit. Nothing to do with what he'd been smoking. That day, a part of him lit up, a part he'd no idea was there to light. He had felt a sharp stabbing sensation, right there in the flat part between his ribs, in his solar plexus.

"Come back, nuh," he said, soft soft and gentlemanlike after his mother-tears had dried and his face was tight with the salt. Something had happened. She had risen from the waves, chosen him, a humble fisherman.

"Come, nuh, *dou dou*," he pleaded, this time softer still, as if to lure her. But the water had settled back flat.

Next morning, David went to the exact same spot by those jagged rocks off Murder Bay and waited for several hours and saw nothing. He smoked nothing. Day after, the same thing. Four days he went out to those rocks in his pirogue. He cut the engine, threw out the anchor, and waited. He told no one what he had seen. He avoided Ce-Ce's parlour, the property of his kindhearted, bigmouth aunt. He avoided his cousins, his pardners in St. Constance. He went home to his small house on the hill, the house he'd built himself, surrounded by banana trees, where he lived with Harvey, his pot hound. He felt on edge. He went to bed early so as to rise early. He needed to see the mermaid again, to be sure that his eyes had seen correctly. He needed to cool what had become an inflammation in his heart, to pacify the buzz that had started up in his nervous system. He had never had this type of feeling, certainly not for no mortal woman.

Then, day five, around six o'clock, he was strumming his guitar, humming a hymn, when the mermaid showed herself again.

This time she splashed the water with one hand and made a sound like a bird squeak. When he looked up he didn't frighten so bad, even though his belly clenched tight and every fibre in his body froze. He stayed still and watched her good. She was floating port side of his boat, cool cool, like a regular woman on a raft, except there was no raft. The mermaid, with long black hair and big, shining eyes, was taking a long suspicious look at him. She cocked her head, and it was only then David realised she was watching his guitar. Slow slow, so as not to make her disappear again, he picked it up and began to strum and hum a tune, quietly. She stayed there, floating, watching him, stroking the water, slowly, with her arms and her massive tail.

The music brought her to him, not the engine sound, though she knew that too. It was the magic that music makes, the song that lives within every creature on earth, including mermaids. She hadn't heard music for a long time, maybe a thousand years, and she was irresistibly drawn up to the surface, real slow and real interested.

That morning David played her soft hymns he'd learnt as a boy, praising God. He sang holy songs for her, songs which brought tears to his eyes, and there they stayed, on this second meeting, a small patch of sea apart, watching each other—a young, wet-eyed Black Conch fisherman with an old guitar, and a mermaid who'd arrived on the currents from Cuban waters, where once they talked of her by the name of Aycayia.

———

I disappear one night, in a big storm
long long ago
Island once where Taino people live
and the people before Taino
North in this pattern of islands and west too
The island I remember
was shaped like a lizard
I have seen the sea
I have seen its glory
I have seen its power
the power of its kingdom
I have swum its angers
I have swum its misery
I have swum its velvet floor

the corals
the cities underneath
I have swum under islands
I have swum close to shore in shallow waves
and seen children playing
I have swum with slow steel canoa
I have swum everywhere in this archipelago
I have swum with large POD of dolphins
I have swum with SHOAL of fish
big like the size of one whole human being
I have dived into walls of ocean
I would have died very soon as a woman
Forty cycles? Children, husband
life of land and life of birth and death
Instead I lived for more than a thousand cycles
inside the sea
I was not alone at the time of my cursing
an old woman was also cursed
and she disappeared too same night
long long ago so long I don't know the time
only that they called up a huracan
to take me far away
seal up my legs inside a tail

―――

David Baptiste's journal, March 2015

Whenever I see the first leatherbacks arrive, I always feel happy.
I know she, my mermaid, will soon appear, happy too, to greet
me. I used to look out for she every evening from April onwards.
She always knew where to find me, by the same jagged rocks

where we first ketch sight of each other, one mile off Murder Bay. Still a private place, even now, since all the damn fish in the sea get fished out. I look out for Aycayia more than half mih damn life. I have plenty women since those days long past, all kinda woman—friend, babymother, lover—but nothing ever again like she.

She was something else.

I am an ol' man now, and sick sick so I cyan move much, sick so I cyan work, go out to sea, and so I go write my story. I go sit down and drink a rum or two to drown my sorrow, drown my damn fuckin heart in this bottle. After Hurricane Rosamund, everything changed, man, every last damn thing blow away and then, one year on from the time we meet, yeah, she come back!

Miss Rain teach she words in that time she came by me, after they pull she out of the sea that fateful day. She know language of her own, and some of these words came out in our sexing. But it was a long-ago language and her memory of it wasn't strong. She hadn't spoken it for so very long. While we lived together, we learn the name of every fish, she and me, from the same encyclopedia that belong to Miss Rain. I would take it out in my boat. Aycayia like to learn and she wanted to know the name of every fish in the whole damn ocean, everything in the sea and along the shore. I learn half those names myself—and every fish have a Latin name too. So all now she is a mermaid who know the names of every damn fish in the sea in two languages, an some she can call in she own tongue.

The mermaid scare me like hell when I first see her. Her top half pop up from the sea. She was red, like an Amerindian woman, and all scaly and glittery too, like she polish sheself up good. Up she came from nowhere, man. I heard a splash and then *woosh*.

Up she rise. She appreciate them hymns I was singing that day. Turned out she like the sound of my voice, how it carry over the water. Later I came to understand she arrived at our shores from Cuban waters. Only much later did she tell me her strange story and her name. She travel down from there on the currents with an old woman, Guanayoa. I remember how she was curious about the encyclopedia. What name I have, she ask. How come I don't have a picture in there?

Over the next few weeks, I saw her maybe every day. She got to know the sound of the motor on my boat. Like she was waiting. I was careful about pissing in the water. I brought an old jerry can for that. I decided to be patient and so I sat and wait for she, long hours. Next thing, I see one big tail fin, big like a pilot whale. My heart felt warm. She opened my heart, one time, that mermaid, Lawd. She made my heart swell up in my chest, just like that. She open my mind, too, to other animals and fish we don't know about. She use to swim the sea sad sad, or so she say, before we met. I ent know how she survive all those years in that big ocean, all alone. She had to be brave for that, though she was fraid of me, when we met, of what I might do if I ketch her good. She and I lock eyes many times, in wonder at each other, before them Americans catch her.

One time, when we first meet, she swam close to my boat. I saw her real good then. Her head was smooth smooth, delicate, small eyes, small face. She looking like a woman from long ago, like old-time Taino people I saw in a history book at school. She face was young and not pretty at all, and I recognise something ancient there too. I saw the face of a human woman who once lived centuries past, shining at me. I saw she breasts, under the fine scaly suit. I saw webbed fingers and how they dripped with sargassum seaweed. Her hair was full of seaweed too, black

black and long and alive with stinging creatures—like she carry a crown on her head of electricity wires. Every time she raise up her head I watch her hair fly up, like she ketch fire-coral inside it.

Then, there was her tail. Oh Laa-aad-o. The things a man could see, especially if he connect with nature, and live close to the sea.

I saw that part of this creature from my boat. Yards and yards of musty silver. It gave she a look of power, like she grow out of the tail itself. I think, then, that this fish-woman must be heavy as a mule. She must weigh four or five hundred pounds, easy. When I see her first, I reckon she come from some half-space in God's great order, like she was from a time when all creatures were getting designed. She was from when fish was leaving the sea behind, growing legs, turning into reptiles. She was a creature that never make it to land. Is what I was thinking before I hear she own story. I figure she and she kind get interrupted somewhere in the middle of God's act of creation.

I was a young fella back then. I never stop to think I could make trouble for she. Man already make her miserable, women curse her good: that's how she end up a mermaid in the sea, condemn to loneliness and her sex seal up inside a big tail. That was what them women had in mind, to keep her away from their men. After I rescue her, I never imagine she could get hurt again, by man or by me. Many times I sing and play my guitar to her off them rocks in Murder Bay. I never bother dropping my lines after seeing her the second time, 'cause I fraid of hooking her. Was my fault, though, they ketch her, them Yankee men. My fault. She thought she heard the engine sound of my pirogue, *Simplicity*. I was there with them, and so she follow their boat by accident.

2

Dauntless

≈≈≈

WHEN THE BIG BOSTON WHALER, by the name of *Dauntless*
from Florida, arrived in late April 1976, in time for the annual
Black Conch fishing competition, its owners, two white men,
Thomas and Hank Clayson, were looking for crew. Nicer
Country was recommended to them as a local expert on the
currents around the island. He was a fisherman of some note.
Only the year before he'd brought in a six-hundred-pound
marlin and that beast of a fish, spike and all, had made a photograph on the front page of the *Gazette*. So they hired him as
captain. Nicer, in turn, hired two local boys as crew, Short Leg
and Nicholas, brothers from different fathers, whose mother,
a bite-up woman by the name of Priscilla, was a neighbour of
David's up in the hill behind the village.

Over the next few days more and more fishing boats started
to arrive: *Sea Sprite, Pilar, August Moon, Divine Flight, Tabanca, Jou-
vay, Mariner's Dream*. Most came down the chain of islands from
as far as Bimini and the Bahamas. Others came from Grenada,
St. Kitts, Nevis, and Martinique. They came from the Florida

Keys too, also from Venezuela and Trinidad. One boat even came from Colombia. All were looking to land blue marlin, swordfish, sailfish, tarpon and shark. Every boat was like a team from the owner down—with a captain and crew they either brought with them or hired locally. Every man jack in St. Constance was looking to make money. Some of the local men had adapted their vessels with outriggers and bait boxes. Some had bought bigger engines. By the last week in April, forty or fifty boats had arrived and were anchored in Murder Bay.

Friday evening before the first fishing day, Ce-Ce's parlour was humming. Chalkdust and the Mighty Sparrow were jamming from the speakers in the roof. Everybody liming, drinking, talking, eating flying fish and fresh hot bake, saltfish fritters and French fries. Every Black Conch fisherman and boy was there to maco the other boats in the bay. Ce-Ce herself had been in the kitchen all day with her helpers, making curry goat and roti skins. Ce-Ce, with her loud, hoarse laugh, and hips so wide she always walked through doors sideways, said she felt sure of a good catch, that she would be serving fried fish for the whole next month.

The two white men were father and son. Thomas Clayson, the father, dressed himself in khaki shorts and fishermen's rubber boots. He wore a soiled captain's hat over what was left of his hair and he wheezed on an old cigar. He was already very red in the face from his trip down from Miami. Hank, the son, wore a safari hat and a yellow T-shirt with the words FORTUNE FAVOURS THE BOLD. His white socks were snug under his leather sandals and his legs were thin and pale. A selection of penknives dangled from his belt.

Saturday, daybreak, April 24, 1976, the whaler *Dauntless* set out ahead of the other boats. It was perfect conditions for a fishing competition. The sea was flat and turquoise in the shallows, purple in the deep. No winds expected; dry season, an early mango season, the start of hill-fire season. No rain for weeks.

David's pirogue *Simplicity* trailed behind the whaler, his engine making a loud *chugalug* sound, the prow of the boat slicing the water. He had decided to accompany them, for a short while, out of curiosity, and also out of fear of what they might catch. He hadn't seen his mermaid friend for a few days and he'd assumed, and hoped, dearly hoped, she'd swum away.

Aboard the whaler, there were five men: Thomas, the captain; Hank, the son; Nicer; and Short Leg and his half brother Nicholas. The bait from the outriggers was two succulent squid, trailing and dipping and curling up in the waves; each was fresh and tantalising to anything with an appetite below. The two white men sat in the fighting chairs, staring hard out to sea. What they were thinking that day, God alone knows. Some say they were frightened. Some say they were confident. All agree they didn't know Black Conch waters, let alone its ways. The old man, they say, had failed at everything he had tried in his life.

A shoal of flying fish rose and sped on their fins next to the boat, a sign there was something bigger chasing them. Nicer was up on the flying bridge, his eyes peeled, his hands on the gear stick. There was a feeling of awkwardness between the men. The white men made it clear they'd no time for polite talk, that they had nothing to say to each other, let alone their crew. They were unsure of themselves and what might happen. So each of the men on board gazed outwards at the sea, and felt alone and inside himself. The sea, that expanse of nothingness, could reflect a man back on himself. It had that effect. It was so endless and it moved around underneath the boat. It wasn't the same thing at all as being on any expanse of earth. The sea shifted. The sea could swallow the boat whole. The sea was the giant woman of the planet, fluid and contrary. All the men shuddered as they gazed at her surface. Even Nicer could feel his balls shrink and his pores raise. Blue open water, they called it. Nicer didn't like the look of these white men at all. Hank, the younger one, began to sing and his father growled and cut him dead. They didn't trust, let alone like, each other. The sky was transparent, not a cloud, not an angel formation in sight. The sun dripped down on them, like acid. Not a sea bird called, not another boat to look at. It put the men in a low mood. The sea reflected back their very souls.

An hour passed, maybe more. The sea said, *Be careful what you ask for. I am bigger than you. Take only what you need.* The men were, frankly, mesmerised by the time it all happened.

They all saw it, at once—a large boil of water under the surface; something large had taken the bait starboard side. The line fell from the outrigger in a long slow loop that became tight the minute it hit the water.

"Fish!" shouted Thomas Clayson. "Goddamn."

Both white men had the butts of their rods in the gimbals. All the men could feel the pull, but couldn't see the fish. The line was now racing out at a slant, cutting into the water. Something big had taken the bait and was swimming away with it fast. The line was going down, and it was the line attached to the younger Clayson's rod. The rod bowed and the Black Conch men rushed to help him into the harness. Hank Clayson braced his feet against the stern, his hands shook and he hollered, "Dad, it's on mine. It's on my rod." The rod was bowed to the sea so steeply it looked like it would snap or fly out of the gimbal.

Nicer Country knew what to do: keep the fish astern, at all costs, or else the line would snap. He revved the motors down, so they were barely turning over. Hank Clayson's rod was bent double and the line was still going rapidly out. The young man was leaning back on his rod. Nicer turned the boat in a small circle so as to get the fish behind them. They all watched as the line travelled out and down, as if a horse was running with it, all of them knowing that they'd struck lucky; they'd got what they came for.

"I think it's a billfish," said Hank, who, in truth, knew nothing at all about fish; this was his first trip.

"It's a blue marlin, to be sure, a female, by the weight of it," said the father.

The crew stood still on deck, watching the line run and run, all of them chilled to the marrow. This was only the strike; the fight was to come. The young man Hank held back on his rod and watched as the line continued to move out and out at an angle to the boat.

"Pull back now," shouted Thomas Clayson. "Now, hit it hard."

This flustered the son and he began to tug backwards, pulling and making no difference at all to the line. The fish was heading farther out.

"What if it just has the bait in its mouth?" said Hank. "What if it's just taking us out, playing with us, not hooked at all?"

"Fish ain't that smart," said the father. "It's hooked to be sure."

"What if the fish spits out the bait?"

"It won't."

Hank Clayson braced his feet and tightened the drag on his rod and struck back hard against the weight of the fish. The line continued to move out. He was making no impression at all. Lines of sweat trickled down the sides of his face. He had forgotten to put on sun cream and was turning tomato red.

"Hit him again," the father said. "Go on now, put your elbow into it, and pull back."

The crew men watched, aghast. The young man's efforts were making no purchase. The line was heading out into the deep. Hank Clayson bent back again and there was a sharp zizzing sound on the line and the rod was now so bent towards the sea he could hardly keep hold of it. Nicer slowly turned the boat, keeping the fish aback of it. Nicer guessed that the son was a beginner and he'd hooked something too big to be starting with. Short Leg and Nicholas knew it too.

Nicer realised this was going to take some time.

David was some way behind in his pirogue. He was puffing on a spliff and wasn't yet aware they'd caught anything.

For an hour they laboured with the fish. Every man wanted to take over from Hank; every man wished he could be the one with the rod, but it would be wrong to interfere. The line on Hank's rod continued to fall off the reel.

"Work on him, Hank," said the father, annoying his son.

The fish wasn't tired; it was still running with the line. Hank lowered the rod and lifted it, lowered it and lifted it as best he could. In truth, he wished he could give the rod away to another man on the boat; this trip hadn't been his idea of fun. It had been some kind of gift, his father's idea of bonding. Now he'd hooked something, his stomach was a mess of knots.

"Stay with her," said the father. The fish was sounding now, diving deep, frightened and making a desperate bid to change

direction. Nicer backed the boat very slowly to ease the pressure
on the line.

"Jesus, it's practically towing the boat," said Hank.

———

A juicy squid ketch me
Who coulda believe a squid could be so vicious?
My mouth was on fire in one sudden time
I feel tight lash and pull back
I think I hear *Simplicity* chug chug sound
I swim away fast fast but hook inside ketch me good

I swim deep deep for a long time
down, down to the floor of the ocean
It was not *Simplicity* but
Yankee man boat at the end of the line
At first I think I could take the boat
to the ocean floor
but the Yankee men
have big big boat

Frighten bad I swim down down
towards ocean's safety
in the black deep sea parts
Something strong on the surface pulling me back
My throat was on fire with hurt
I was strangling myself
I was drowning in the sea
I jump up high to show them they had caught me

Me a human fish
Let me go

You make a mistake
I swim down and deep long time
I knew there was no hope
no survival
I swam towards my dying

David oh them Yankee men catch me
when I thought it was you
They ketch me good
David where are you?
You are not there any more
Please find this letter I put in a bottle

———

Hank Clayson was turning purple in the sun.

"It's getting tired now," said Thomas Clayson. "Get some water for his head, or he'll die of sunstroke catching this fish."

Short Leg went to the bait box, which was full of ice; dipped in a bucket; brought it back; and tipped some of the ice water on the son's head. It was true that white men could die from sunburn; Short Leg had heard the stories. White men fraid nothing more than too much sun; too much sun could end up making him a dead man. They could pass out, get a heart attack. Short Leg doused the youth's head good with the ice water from the bucket. He enjoyed seeing him flinch.

The fish was now tiring, but it had taken almost every piece of the line, and Hank Clayson was aching all over from holding the rod. He hurt bad in his shoulders and arms.

"Pretty soon the fish will have to come up," said Thomas Clayson, biting on his cigar. He was a man who'd seen some action at sea. He'd brought his son here to make a man of him. But his son didn't seem to care that much about being a man. He was a goddamn sissy, reading books. Now and then he even wrote 'poems.' Clayson had sent him to an expensive law school, but the boy had disappointed him even in that, saying he was going to defend the poor, the single mothers, immigrants. His plans for his son had backfired. His son was 'sensitive,' his wife had said. Like a frigging plant. Now his son had hooked a fish that might even weigh a thousand pounds. Thomas Clayson wished it was him who had the fish on the end of his rod; his son wouldn't cope once the fish started to fight. His son had only been holding the fish while it moved out to sea. Very soon, he would have to start reeling it in. And yet he wanted his son to catch the fish, wanted that more than anything on earth; it would be a fine thing. Imagine the pride of having a son capable of such a conquest.

By then, *Dauntless* was so far out to sea that David had turned *Simplicity* back towards home. He went back to drink a rum at Ce-Ce's parlour, trying to quell his fears.

On the whaler, Hank Clayson, in the fighting chair, braced his feet against the stern and pulled on the rod using all his body weight. He lowered the rod and then reeled, lowered and reeled. Steadily, the line was coming in, one inch, then two inches at a time, more and more line was coming back in.

"This is one bitch of a fish," he said. "I can't wait to see it."

The Black Conch boys poured ice water on his head again.

"It's easier now, holding her steady."

"Don't work it any faster than you can," said Thomas Clayson.

All five men were now full of anticipation. More than an hour had passed. The fish was tired. They were winning. All they needed to do now was keep the boat straight and slowly reel the fish in.

"Can you get me a Coke?" Hank said. "I'm real thirsty."

The line had begun to slant down deep into the water.

"Watch it, Hank," the father said. "It'll come up any minute."

Hank Clayson could feel it too, that the fish was about to jump. Nicer began to back the boat up.

"The thing's about to come up," shouted the father. "Son of a goddamn bitch is coming up. Keep your rod up!"

The flat dark sea broke open. The mermaid rose up and out of the water, her hair flying like a nest of cables, her arms flung backwards in the jump, her body glistening with scales and her tail flailing, huge and muscular, like that of a creature from the deepest part of the ocean. She beat up and out, arcing through the air so she flipped on her back. The men saw her head, her breasts, her belly, the pubic bone of a woman where it met the tail of a glistening fish.

"Jesus Christ!" exclaimed Thomas Clayson.

Nicer crossed himself.

The Black Conch boys gasped.

"Cut de line!" shouted Nicer Country. "Cut de goddamn line."

All five men were horrified as she hit the water, thrashing. Her mouth was bloody and she'd only just started to fight. On the end of Hank Clayson's rod was a wild creature, furious to be caught.

Nicer knew they'd hooked something they shouldn't have. He jumped down from the flight bridge with his knife. The mermaid, or whatever it was, deserved to stay in the sea. This wasn't his business at all. The thing looked too big for the boat. It could take the boat down, even.

"Don't do that," shouted Thomas Clayson, as Nicer bent to cut the line. "DO NOT do that. She's worth millions. Millions. We're bringing her in, goddamn it. We are bringing her in."

She was on the surface now, thrashing like a mako shark, fighting the line with her arms, coughing up blood and spitting and screaming a high wailing song.

"Oh God," stammered Hank. "Did you see that?" His hands were shaking on the rod.

The father wanted to take it from him. The Black Conch men, Nicholas and Short Leg, backed away from the stern. Like Nicer, they knew this was wrong. They fraid bad jumbie get ketch. They didn't want to help. They were lost for words and for what to do. The white men wanted to pull this creature out of the sea. But this fish was half-woman, plain enough. Everyone had heard of the mermen in Black Conch waters, but a merwoman? No. She carried with her bad luck, at best, and her hair had frightened them—like she could kill with just one lash from those tentacles. She could poison them all. They'd seen spikes on her back, dorsal spikes. Scorpion fish spikes. They had seen a bloody, raging woman on the end of the fishing line and now these white men wanted to bring her in. *Nah, boy*, they all said to themselves.

The mermaid was now under the surface again. The younger Clayson's face was full of terror and excitement.

"Hold her," shouted the father.

"What does it look like I'm doing," the son snapped.

"Keep backing up on it," Thomas Clayson shouted to Nicer.

Nicer had begun to see dollar signs. If it had been him alone, he would have thrown her back in the sea, but the talk made him realise this could make him enough money for another boat, a new car, a small business of his own. Imagine that. He threw the throttle into reverse and slowed the boat down. The engine hummed. Nicer could feel his own curiosity grow. How much would she fetch? He backed the boat slowly onto the fish. The line had stopped going out. The younger Clayson was lifting and lowering his rod, lifting and lowering and the line was now coming back onto the reel as fast as he could turn the reel handle. The mermaid had gone back under, for now.

"That thing must weigh six hundred pounds," said Thomas Clayson. The ocean was flat and empty again. There was silence apart from the sound of the reel ticking over.

"Did you see her?" said Hank Clayson.

"Hell, yes," said the father.

"Did you see her tits?" said the son. He was so entranced by what he'd caught, it had loosened his tongue.

"Hell, yes."

"Did you see her face?"

"Yes."

"Did you see her arms?"

"Yes."

"Did you see her . . . pussy bone?"

All the men nodded at this.

"We could sell her to the Smithsonian," said Thomas Clayson. "Or the Rockefeller Institute. For research."

The line was slowly coming in. For the next twenty minutes, the men stared hard astern, each calculating what might happen if they caught her and each feeling a deep boiling-up sensation in his groin. They didn't know what to expect. They kept their eyes on the sea, and listened to the reel ticking. She was coming in, but she would fight again.

"Be careful we don't end up over her," said Thomas.

Nicer knew that could happen; he revved the engine again.

"Tighten on her, a little," said the father.

Hank Clayson had been holding the rod and the weight of the mermaid for almost two hours and his whole body was aflame with the strain of it.

The line started to go out again.

"Let the motor idle."

Nicer stopped the engine.

Then the boat started to move backwards. Hank Clayson was reeling her in, but the shorter the line got, the more she pulled back. There was a creaking sound, somewhere in the boat's hull. She was pulling back on the line. She must weigh the same as another small boat, Nicer thought. If she got under the hull, she could take *Dauntless* down.

Minutes ticked past. The ocean was quiet. Metallic blue. *Take only what you need*, she whispered.

"Shit," said Thomas Clayson. "She's under the boat."

They waited and watched. Slowly, a large shadow passed beneath them, something big. One flip of its back and they could be pitched upwards, into the air. Thomas Clayson unstrapped himself from his harness, stood up and peered deep and whistled.

The sea broke open again.

She jumped, port side.

This time, she was more fish than woman and her power was clear. She leaped high and wide of the boat, her tail gleaming like yards of wide silver ribbon. Up she breached and her mass of clotted dreads flew and her bloodied mouth was twisting with the line. She came down heavily in the water, causing a mighty wake, slapping the water with her tail. The boat fell a good two inches port side. She swam hard and took the boat with her. The Black Conch men were shouting to cut the line. Thomas Clayson panicked too, for to rev the engine against her would mean to snap the line and lose her.

The mermaid dove deep, and the boat tipped and the men fell on top of each other, except for Hank, who was harnessed into the chair.

"Fight her," shouted the father. "Bring that bitch in."

The boat lurched again. Then it rolled as if its very belly had been tugged, as if the mermaid might be able to tug away the flybridge, or the aft deck, as if she might be able to pull the boat apart.

The reel zizzed.

Hank Clayson's rod was bent into the sea. It was clear he couldn't hold it. He was too tired and his will had flagged. He was frightened now of what he'd caught. The boat was moving backwards and it was listing badly. They were far out at sea, no sight of land.

The father grabbed the rod from his son and he began to show his skill as a fisherman. He had caught big game fish before; he wasn't frightened. He knew there was an hour or two to come. They had only just started this struggle. The mermaid was tired and yet she was also strong.

"Get me a drink," said Thomas Clayson to no one in particular. "There's a flask of rum in the satchel. Bring it to me."

Nicer began to see the course of events. Man against catch to the bitter end; man against creature and the creature was half-woman. The old white man exchanged seats with his son and strapped himself into the harness. Short Leg brought him his flask of rum. The boat belonged to this man; he'd come to show his sissy-assed son how to fish. Now he'd stepped in.

"Rev the engine just a touch," he said to Nicer.

———

My lungs fill up with water
but I know the sea better than Yankee men
Woman put me in the sea
Call for huracan

Now man want to take me out
I feel fresh pain
Next man pulling on the line
The hook in my throat
I want to go down to die

Or I could turn their canoa over
and pitch the men out
I was a very big fish
I was heavy
I would swim with the current
Current strong enough
then I could do it

I swam away, then dive deep
My terror was ENORMOUS
I swam but I still ketch
I want to go down to die

Enough shame put on my head
I was a human woman once
some thousand cycles past
Cursed to be lonely
with no love
They curse me good
Goddess Jagua was the goddess of their curse
She keep me lonely all those years

I miss my life in Black Conch
I was human woman again
after they ketch me good

––––––

Thomas Clayson swigged deep on his flask. Nicholas and Short Leg took turns in pouring ice water on his head. The younger Clayson was burnt to a crisp and had lost his nerve completely, though he'd done most of the work. He'd poured some of the rum from the flask onto his chafed and bleeding hands. They were in the third hour of the fight. Thomas Clayson started to work on the rod. He set his feet on the stern, saying nothing, saving his breath as he worked, pumping, lowering, raising and reeling in the line. On the fly-deck Nicer kept the engine humming, moving forward slowly. The line was as taut as it could be without snapping.

"She's damned strong," said Thomas Clayson. "Strong as six men."

Then the line started to go out again. Clayson shut his eyes, braced his feet and hung back on the rod. The creature was circling the boat. Even though they had gained significant line, the line was going out again, steadily. It was sounding again; it had come close to the surface and then gone deep down.

"It may be going deep to try and die," said Nicholas. These were the first words he'd spoken all day. The young Black Conch man had been deeply troubled by what he'd seen. His cousin Nicer Country had got him involved in the fishing competition. He figured it might earn him some money so he could take his girlfriend to check a film in English Town.

"I figure she go deep to die. She trying to drown sheself."

"Shut up," said Thomas Clayson.

The men all stood back and watched. The line was going out again, but slower now.

The old man began to pump and reel, pump and reel. He knew he was going to have the thing; he knew he was going to win. He'd caught many big fish and he understood, deep down, the nature of this game: that this was always an unfair fight. While there was a skill to reeling in a game fish, there was no skill at all in the odds. A broadbill would fight way against its weight. But it had no chance, which wasn't the point. It was the game of it he loved. The patience of it, the thrill, the sight of the catch. Never mind the odds. He'd never lost a fish yet. But this was different. This was going to make him and his family famous. He could hardly wait to see her strung up on the jetty. Imagine the photograph on the cover of *LIFE* magazine, *National Geographic*; the news would go round the world. He would be able to command an auction. This was his endgame, enough money for him to retire.

The line went tight again and he lowered the rod. It bent so much it was doubled like a rainbow, and yes, yes, he could start to see the top of her again. She was swimming fast now, towards the boat, against her will, well and truly hooked; all he needed to do now was to reel and lower, reel and lower. Soon it would be time to get her on the boat.

"Get the gaff ready," he said, but none of the men came forward. It would take all of them and she would fight. And then there was the hair, lethal, the dreadlocks of a man o' war.

Eventually, they had her alongside the boat, bloody and tired and seemingly almost the length of *Dauntless*. So close, she was terrifying, a person there, no doubt about it; a trapped and dying woman under the water, her long tail moving slowly, her fins working like gentle propellers, a cloud of blood blossoming from her mouth. The local men stared. They felt a sense of blasphemy; this was something they shouldn't be doing. They should pull the hook from her mouth and release her back into the deep. They saw her rare nature, her long dreadlocks flowing about her, and the water jolting electric currents of silver alongside her tail.

"Bring her up," said Thomas Clayson.

They managed to get a rope around her tail fin and the old man himself reached down low with the gaff hook and stabbed in deep and the mermaid throbbed and writhed.

Four of them hauled her up by the gaff and the rope and in the end she came in with gallons of water and other fish, a giant *woosh* and the boat deck was full of her. She was half dead already, from the hours of swimming against them with the hook in her throat and now the steel gaff in her flank. She was bleeding heavily, stunned, grunting, her tinfoil eyes watching them.

Her hair was the worst part, a mess of fire and ropes of this and that. Jellyfish had come up with her, clusters of long blue veins. Sea moss trailed from her shoulders like slithers of beard. Barnacles speckled the swell of her hips. Her torso was sturdy and muscular, finely scaled over, as if she wore a tunic of sharkskin. She was crawling with sea-lice. They saw that when her diaphragm heaved, it revealed wide slits which were gills and they looked sharp enough to slice a finger off. All the men backed away. Her spine spikes were flat, like the spokes of a folded umbrella, but when they flared and spread, they revealed a mighty dorsal.

"Holy Lord," Nicer whispered.

The mermaid lay there, heaving and bleeding. They heard the loud sounds of her gasps. The men stared. Everyone felt it, the sadness of her existence, a woman who'd been alone in the sea. Had she jumped from a boat? Had her mother mated with a fish? Every man could feel his heart pounding hard in his chest, with fear and a sense of wonderment, at this half and half. Her eyes flicked over them, full of stark contempt. She'd fought hard to stay in the ocean. Each man felt a deep tug in his crotch. The old man wanted to take out his dick and piss all over her. The younger men fought hard to keep a cockstand from bouncing up in their pants. She was like a magnet. She was a woman hooked, clubbed, half-dead, half-naked and virgin young. Each man could see to she, for sure. She was spitting up seawater; it seemed to be flowing out of her from deep in her gullet. Water seeped from her gills. She was a fish out of water, and yet she wasn't going to expire like an ordinary fish. She was taking in big fast gulps of air like a thirsty child, trying to stay alive. Her hair was moving, spreading itself across the deck. Numerous pilot fish were dying off around her. She already looked smaller than when she was in the sea.

"Pour some rum in her gills," said Short Leg.

"No. That might kill her," said the old man. "Tie up her arms."

The younger Black Conch men quailed, they backed away. Neither wanted to go near her and yet she was now inside the vessel, her tail thumping the deck. She was a fish and a woman welded together. All they could do was stare, in shock. Her tail was curvaceous and strong and shot through with oily rainbow colours. Her hands were frilled with webbing. The webbing dripped with bracelets of mother of pearl. When she opened her hands, her fingers were bony and thin; the webbing glowed pink and opalescent.

"I want you," Short Leg whispered, repulsed. He touched his mouth.

Nicer knew they were a long way from land, that they'd just enough gas to get them back, but this wasn't the kind of thing he felt comfortable bringing back home. Imagine the picong, the bad behaviour of his pardners when they saw this half-fish, half-woman, imagine the ruckus she was going to cause.

Hank and Thomas Clayson had tied her hands and gagged her mouth. They drank cold beers. Hank took photos of her on his Kodak Polaroid. Each one stooped, grinning, next to her sullen face. Her teeth biting into the rope. She was scared. Her shock was palpable and yet she drew no remorse from the American men. Not the father, anyway. His eyes were bugged out, and he couldn't stop gaping at his catch. What a thing to pull from the sea. Some kind of freak. He would keep her alive in a tank, fly her home. He gloated at his son. Young Hank Clayson was still a virgin, truth be told. He hadn't learnt the manly skills needed to trap a woman into a dinner date, let alone marriage. Hank had watched other men not even have to try, the high school jocks, and, over time, he'd given up. He was an aesthete. He read the classics, albeit in translation. One day, there would be a different type of woman in his life, one who would understand him. And now this. They had pulled a woman from the sea. Like the other men, it gave him a deep-rooted charge in his prick. Maybe big game fishing was exciting after all; maybe he would even try it again. For the first time ever, he'd hooked a woman. He would write poems about the mermaid they'd just captured, a crown of sonnets perhaps. He would do his best to commemorate her, his first woman, his Helen of Atlantis, his water-maiden.

They poured red rum on her hair to quiet it down. Then they hooded her face with an old piece of tarp, so she couldn't look at them with those silver-black, hate-filled eyes.

The journey back was mostly silent. The sun was going to drop in the next hour. The mermaid had begun to make an incessant moaning sound. Her body flipped and thudded back and forth and they'd begun to worry she could even jump out of the boat. Thomas Clayson hit her hard over the head with the metal lure box and knocked her out.

"Get us home," he ordered Nicer.

The sea looked quiet on the way back; the clouds were gathered down low on it, lit behind by the failing sun, their edges pink. The men all sank deep into their own thoughts. Nicer was thinking of his bed, his woman, his home and his life, how content he'd been that morning. He'd even grown to like the tiny wooden home he'd been renting with his wife for many years off Miss Arcadia Rain. Now, it felt like everything was different, like he'd committed a crime. He should never have taken this job from a white man he hadn't liked on sight. He'd been a fisherman all his life. From the age of seventeen he had worked the sea, gone out before dawn, returning before midday. A daily routine and it had been a livelihood. He'd seen a few things. Once, he'd caught a rare dappled grouper the size of a small calf; it had taken three men to get it from the boat onto the back of a truck bound for English Town. The fish had taken over an hour to die. It had finally been sawn up into thick rubbery steaks on the wharf, sold to one of the big hotels. He had caught sharks, and he'd caught leatherbacks too, and all kinds of ray, almost everything there is to catch—a big marlin the year before. He'd seen fishermen go out and come back in twice a day from the time he could ever remember anything. On the foreshore there was a stone depot and he'd grown up around it, boy and man. His father fished. Every other man in the north of Black Conch was a fisherman. But even though he'd heard the mermen stories, he'd never seen anything like this half-and-half thing they ketch today. He didn't like that she was half-naked, half-female. He didn't like her glittery, hard-looking eyes, didn't like that she had seen him. Her grunts—they sounded as though they had captured something female, like his mother or his sister or an aunt, like she might even be able to say something once she caught her breath.

When they hauled their catch onto the jetty she was still gagged, bound, and unconscious. She was breathing, but shallowly. She had turned a different colour. The shine had dulled from her tail. It was already turning brown. It looked as though her body was now covered in dank and peeling wallpaper. Maybe she would die. Maybe she was dying. She had certainly grown smaller. There were two blue marlin lynched by their tails already on the jetty, large as racks of beef. Many boats were in, moored. Men were milling about; they were at the bar, having a rum or three at Ce-Ce's. The sun was setting.

They strung her up alongside the two marlin for all to see, her head hanging downwards, her deadly hair trailing, her arms lashed with rope behind her back, her breasts naked. Many men crowded round and they all wanted to touch her and some of them did. They poked and pinched her tail, testing it. One put his fingers out and touched her rough belly skin.

"Hey, cutie," he said, nervous.

Men laughed.

One went further and tweaked her nipples, which were hard as nubs of stone.

She writhed at his touch.

Though she had shrunk, she was still bigger than the marlin. No one knew what to say to the Clayson men. Many of the men around just looked on, astonished. Some began to recall mixed-up tales about seeing a merman in Black Conch waters,

though no one had heard of a mermaid in these parts and certainly no other fisherman had ever actually caught one. There
was no phone nearby to call anyone important, like a newspaper
reporter. Someone would have to do that tomorrow. A few of
the foreign fishermen took photographs. Flash bulbs went off.
The mermaid jerked, as if in pain at the flashes. The soft yellow
light of the day was draining from the sky, and the men in the
bar heard the news, and slowly slowly the jetty became crammed
with tired, drunken, salt-skinned fishermen.

Nicer, Short Leg and Nicholas disappeared. Nicer left to a big
pot of pellau, a cold beer and his bed; the other two vanished into
the village behind the bar. None was feeling proud. They would
collect their money the next morning.

It became clear from the talk and the bets and conjecture
of the fishermen that there was a problem. The big game fish
would be weighed and the heads and sword would be removed
as trophies. The fish would go to the depot; they would be gutted
and scaled and sliced and sold. But what of this half-and-half?
What would they do with her?

Was she fish or meat?

Men laughed at the thought of slicing her up.

How much would she fetch by the pound?

Aycayia, the mermaid, dangled upside down, her mouth
bound with rope. Her eyes seeped a type of salt-grease. She
couldn't understand what they were saying, but knew it was
ominous from the jeering tone of their voices. She remembered
men, the ones who'd visited her so often, the husbands, the single
men, all a long time ago. She remembered how they'd come to
hear her songs, watch her dance, how she could barely keep them
away from her; how the women of the village didn't like it at all.

≋

The son, Hank Clayson, was full of sorrow. He'd drunk too many beers too quickly and the fight and the thrill of it and the emotion of the catch now overwhelmed him. His body ached with his hours of holding the rod. He didn't like to see her naked body watched by so many other men. He wanted to cover her up. He wished they hadn't done it now, hadn't pulled her out. Already he was calling her Helen. He didn't know what to do about it all. She was moaning, possibly coming round from the blow to the head. Clearly, no one had any idea what to do about her nakedness, either. Men stared. She was a mutation of the natural world, and she was dying.

Quietly, it started to rain.

One man burped, loudly, and went back into the bar.

Others followed.

Hank Clayson wondered if he would ever be the same again. How could he find a wife for himself after this? The mermaid was supposed to be a 'story' from antiquity. He wanted to cut her down; he wanted to lose the sight of her. He followed the men to the bar, to get damn drunk, drunk as possible.

The rain fell on the mermaid as night settled in. The light at the end of the jetty came on and glowed orange. The rain bathed her. She began to shiver, coming back to life. One man was left to stand guard. Thomas Clayson had stuffed a hundred dollars into his hands and told him he would pay a hundred more when he returned. The guard was a small man with a thick but trimmed moustache and a baseball hat crammed down over his eyes. He was from Miami and had been watching from behind the others. He had been drinking, too, red rum and Coke on ice.

When the others had gone, he took his cigarette from his mouth and stubbed it on her stomach. Then he unbuckled his belt and unzipped his shorts and pulled out his soft pink dick and showed it to her, asking her if she would like to suck it. He'd never had a mermaid suck his dick. He dangled his chubby thing in front of her face as if it were a juicy worm. "See," he said. "Want some?" Then he wiped it across her face and laughed and said that he was the only man on earth to fuck a mermaid and then he grabbed her, and tried to hump her from behind. He would fuck her there and then if he could. He said this loudly into the dead of night and to the mermaid, who'd been approached many times, in her last life, by men who wanted to hump and fuck.

Then, he pissed copiously on her flanks, waving his thing as if to hose her down. His urine was hot and reeked of ammonia and rum.

The mermaid eyed him with utter hatred.

"Go fuck yerself," he said in his Yankee drawl, and then he staggered, drunk, back down the jetty, weaving as he went, towards Ce-Ce's parlour, forgetting he had to keep watch. The parlour was full of men, all still talking about the mermaid. Many stories were told that night, many men had things to say: that they were good luck, that they were bad luck, that they could eat a whole boat, that they had mated with orcas, that they indeed had a clit, a small oyster enfolded somewhere secret in the tail, and everyone laughed at this. Men drank the mermaid down their throats. Thomas Clayson bought drinks on the house. He was dazzled and happy and tired and had a sense that, at last, he had done a great thing near the end of his disappointment of a life. Maybe he would even divorce his wife, finally. He would buy a bigger boat, definitely.

3

Back on Land

≈≈≈

David Baptiste's journal, April 2015

Well, when I saw her hanging upside down, like reverse crucified, my heart stop and my blood run cold cold cold. So, they
ketch her. My worse fear. I kept up with their boat for an hour
or so, but left before they hook her good. They were heading far
out. I turn back; I already had a bad feeling in my gut that my
boat engine might lure her to them. So I turn back, but too late.
My damn fault they pull her out of the sea, bring she back half-
dead. I figure she was dead when I saw her hanging so, upside
down, mouth and hands tie up, just like a crab ready for the
market. I feel shame, man, to see her like that, and I figured
quick quick how to cut her down. I was fraid something bad go
happen otherwise. Men could get on bad in these parts with too
much alcohol, with a thing like this. Miss Rain wouldn't like it at
all. I knew that. She was very particular about women and how
they get treated.

I fetch a wheelbarrow from my neighbour's yard and put it
in the back of my pickup truck and drive down quiet and slow.

Ce-Ce's parlour pack up with fellers liming and drinking and I drove past, recognising half of them. Was lucky that rain coming down. It kept them inside. I drove to the end of the jetty and see her there, hanging next to the big marlin. I think about all the times I saw her in the sea by the rocks off Murder Bay, watching me. All the times we stare each other down. All them times I wonder how God made her and why. The amount of times I say, "Come, dou dou, come, nuh." I hurried fast down the jetty with the wheelbarrow and my cutlass.

Rain coming down even harder then. Her body look cold and dull under the jetty light. Her eyes were closed. But I see her chest rise and fall. I put the barrow under her and with two hard blows to the rope she fell down, half into the barrow. She slump heavy heavy, like a big snake. I knew I had only a few minutes to carry she away. I covered her with a tarp and wheel her to my truck. It was a struggle—taking all my strength to shoulder her fast into the tray.

When I reach home, I bring the hose inside the house and I empty the bathtub of what it have: old boat engine, boat parts, all kind of thing get pelt in there. At the time I would shower with a bucket out back. Same house I still live in now. I build it myself thirty years back, on land Miss Rain say I could buy from her over time. I build the place from wood and concrete that I beg and borrow—that kind of thing, bits and pieces left over from houses my cousins build. Back then, it already have two floors, and a place to cook on a small two-gas burner stove. It have one table, two chairs, one big bed upstairs. No electricity. I used hurricane lamps at night. The tub wasn't even plumbed in. I found it in another person's yard. I figure I could use it one day, and I was right. Of course, Rosamund came and blew most of the house away that year. Little by little, I build it back.

I full the tub to the brim. I emptied one whole box of Saxa salt into it. Only then I start to panic. When I freed the mermaid from the jetty she was still alive. I only had one thing on my mind: to keep her alive overnight. Only God knew what them Yankee men would do with her, sell her to a museum, or worse, Sea World. I wanted to put her back in the sea. I knew I couldn't get her into my boat that same night. I would need help. She was too heavy for me to carry alone from home and then to my boat. First things first. Cut her down. Then I planned to take her in my boat the next night, take her far far out and put her back; I would ask Nicer to help me. Carry she back to the sea, set her free again. I never figure she might stay. All of that was to come. When I first bring she back I ketch my ass just to get her from the tray of the truck into the tub. She was waking up too, in the rain, and I was frighten she might start to beat up.

I carry she like an old roll-up piece of carpet, over one shoulder, and put her in the tub. Then she startled and realise what going on. Her mouth was still gagged and her hands tied up, too, behind her back, but her eyes flew open wide and she start to make loud squawking noises. I put my hand to her mouth and say, "Hush, dou dou. Hush, nuh. Is me, is me, you safe. Safe. Hush."

But she frighten real bad. It took me the rest of the night and half the next day to settle her down in that tub and I didn't untie her hands or mouth till well into the next afternoon, and only when I figured she knew who I was, the rasta man with the guitar who tempted her up from the waves, the one who sang the hymns to the universe.

Eventually, I untied her mouth and she didn't squawk.

"Remember me?" I say.

But she made no sign she knew me at all. She just drink the

water from the tub and lay down low as if she hiding sheself, even though her tail poke out.

She watched me the whole day. Like we'd never met. I was unsure of myself, but I knew I'd have to get her back in the sea. The next day, I untied her hands and still she just lay there flat, flat in the tub, watching me, and I wonder what the hell she was thinking about. Already, I see she tail drying up and she was looking smaller. I poured some rum on a deep wound from the gaff hook near the top of her tail, hoping it would heal up.

When they found the mermaid wasn't hanging there anymore, one set of bacchanal erupted on the foreshore. Thomas Clayson, who was still half-drunk from all his celebrating, bawled *thief!* and instantly raised a reward of fifty thousand US dollars to get her back. The local fishermen knew what happened: jumbie fish already back in the sea, long time. No Black Conch man wanted the reward money; all of them fraid, even before she disappeared. Mermaid gone back into the ocean; she made her own way back. She gone and join the mermen. That was obvious. Only them white men in town was looking for thief. The Black Conch men knew none of them steal her, all of them was cousins and family. How anyone go thief a mermaid and none of them know about it? How any one of them go hide one damn big mudderass mermaid in a small village like St. Constance? She was heavy like a horse. How any one man big enough to cut her down and carry her away? Where people could hide something like that? Nobody have no aquarium at home; nobody have anywhere to keep her. She went back to the sea, joined she breddren; either that, or she get thief by one of them big hotels who send one of their big boats to the jetty while everybody was drunk inside Ce-Ce's. They were already serving she up at Mount Earnest Bay Hotel—that was the talk. A big boat had come and taken her in the night.

All the same, her appearance and disappearance disturbed everyone. When they unlashed the two marlin and took them to the depot and sawed off the heads, something happened which made everybody uneasy. Arnold, the crazyman, behaved crazier than usual. He thiefed the head of one of the marlin and jammed it down on his own head, as if he was playing ol' mas. Then he cavorted around the village wearing the marlin head. He ran around scaring people, shouting and making as if he get ketch too. He kept saying that he was a merman of Black Conch, that he was half-man, half-fish, come to sex with the pretty young women. Imagine that. A man with a long sword-bill on his head. Blood from the marlin's head dripped down his neck all over his shirt and he was running around all morning with his hands all bloody red, threatening to daub them on anyone who got too close. With the spike on his head he looked like a unicorn. Everyone felt bad. Everybody wished the damn mermaid had never been caught and taken to St. Constance. By the time dawn came, a lot of men were suffering from hangover, and, for one reason or another, no one was feeling easy at all.

In time, the news reached up the hill to Miss Arcadia Rain. Her cousin Ce-Ce phoned her about the bacchanal on the foreshore, about the mermaid that appeared and disappeared and the reward for her return, and then about the new merman, Arnold. Miss Rain arrived in her old Land Rover jeep with her son Reggie. He had on his favourite aviator sunglasses and his hair greased into knots. Miss Rain only ever came down to the foreshore in St. Constance if she had to. She mostly lived on her own, up in the great house, where she played the piano and read books. A lot of the fishing boats had already gone out for day two of the competition. Some of them left excited, hoping to re-catch the mermaid. The old man, Thomas Clayson, went back out again, but with different crew, paid double. This time, he swore he'd bring her back, dead. The son, Hank, had refused to go out again. He had been nursing a tabanca for the mermaid, the first woman he ever hooked well and true, and now she was gone, vanished, as magically as she had appeared. He knew he had photographs of her on his camera; that was actual proof, though they weren't really that well focused. His hands must have been shaking. But that morning, it was like the truth of her existence had already come into question. A mermaid that was there and then wasn't was hardly convincing. The *Dauntless* crew had seen her, but now they'd disappeared. The men in the bar had seen her too, but they had quickly gotten drunk and most of them were still asleep. And anyway, who would believe a group of drunken fishermen who said they had seen a mermaid hanging by her tail on the jetty? Ce-Ce hadn't seen her. Nor had her cousin Priscilla, nor had any of the women in the village. Had a bunch of drunkard men made the whole thing up?

So Hank was relieved to see the white woman. He hailed down Miss Rain's jeep in something of a fervour, as if she might be able to call the mermaid back. Maybe Miss Rain had taken her, or knew who had. He was anxious to tell her his story. He was still wearing his yellow T-shirt from the day before, sweat-stained and bloody, though you could still read its inscription FORTUNE FAVOURS THE BOLD. In this faraway Caribbean seaside village Hank Clayson felt laughed at, out of his depth. He wanted to pack his things, ditch the boat and fly back to Miami.

His father had gone mad. He was an embarrassment at the best of times. It was supposed to be a holiday, and now this.

Miss Rain parked and got out of her jeep. She walked towards the young American man, her eyes squinting, reading the words on his T-shirt.

"Hello, ma'am," he said to her in his Florida drawl, "I'm very pleased to meet you."

Miss Rain gave him a look that said he needed a good wash and shave and a good cut ass for getting her out of bed so early on a Sunday morning.

"What de ass been going on here?" she said, ignoring his out-stretched hand, stalking past him towards the jetty. She was in no mood for this—a stupid-looking, young-ass Yankee fisherman, and to boot this story of a mermaid and Arnold with the marlin spike stuck on his head.

Hank soon found that Miss Rain was a hard woman to fathom. For a start, she spoke just like the local fishermen, in the same slow, rhythmic, broken-down, backward English. Even though Hank Clayson had discovered she owned the place, at least all the land around, it was clear she hadn't been educated up. She was white, milk white, in fact, and freckles had exploded across her face and arms, so she looked a little like an appaloosa pony. It was hard not to stare. But her hard green eyes flashed back a *Don't you even dare.* Miss Rain was small, with honey-blonde curly hair cut short like a boy's. It was also clear that she was respected like some kind of mayor. But when she opened her mouth, the same language flowed out, and this was a shock. She was like the Black Conch people, except white. Hank Clayson strode after her, towards the jetty, and towards Arnold, who was sitting on the end of it, still wearing the marlin's spike.

"Arnold," she spoke loudly. "What de hell going on, eh?"

Arnold didn't answer her. He was watching the sea, his legs dangling off the jetty. From behind he looked like a merman, except in reverse.

"Arnold, take that blasted thing off yer head."

Arnold didn't respond.

"Arnold," she repeated, walking closer. "Take that nasty fish head off now. It go give yer a bad case of bacterial infection."

Arnold couldn't hear her. The fish head had blocked his ears.

Miss Rain stood above him. She was wearing flat-heeled sandals and a flowery dress. The man was still staring at the sea in a reverie. This time she didn't ask. She pulled the spiked head up and it came off with a squelch. Arnold gave her a look, as if to ask, why the hell she do that? Miss Rain knew smartman Arnold; they'd met many times before, and truth was, he was probably a cousin, three times removed. She squatted down on her flat heels and said, "Look, nuh, man. Go wash yerself, okay. And stop troubling people."

Arnold shrugged. He didn't need to behave in no particular way for nobody. He was bored. It was said he had once wanted to go to university to study to be a political scientist on the bigger island. Now he was a little crazy from too much ganja smoking and boredom. He liked to frighten people. Miss Rain had figured him out longtime. She had even suggested he go to study, had even offered some money to help. But he hadn't gone because of his ganja habit and because of his collection of caged birds.

"Arnold," she said. "I know you. You know that. Doh waste yuh whole goddamn life making trouble, okay? One thing when you keep trouble to yerself. A whole other thing when you make noise and trouble for everyone else. Okay? I have some work fer yer too, if yuh want. Come and see me some time, okay?"

Arnold nodded but she knew he was indifferent to her bribe. Work. The man was too smart for that.

"Okay, Miss Rain, I'll come up soon." He was lying; he would never come up. He was looking after a good-sized crop of weed up in the hills; a lot of fellers made their living the same way. St. Constance men grew weed or fished the sea. Both hills and sea were abundant in their giving.

"Is you who going an' get trouble," Arnold said.

"What?"

"Trouble coming for you."

"Arnold." And she stopped. "What are you saying?"

"I saw her, you know."

"Saw who?"

"The fish woman."

"Oho, good."

"They strung she up. One tourist man come and behave like a brute."

Miss Rain stared.

"Mami Wata. Looking like they pull some kind of princess from the sea. Should have put her back. She not fer ketch. I not surprise she disappear quick quick."

Miss Rain didn't want to hear any more of this, not now, not so early.

"Is you who own these parts, an you who going an ketch some real trouble if that fish woman is still round here, yuh know? She belong in the sea."

"Okay, then," said Miss Rain. But she had a bad feeling now. She stood up and gazed out over the tranquil bay as she'd done every day of her life. She'd cursed it and loved it. The Rain family had owned almost the whole of St. Constance since 1865, a generation after slavery time. The estate was mostly rain forest high up in the hills, but it came down to St. Constance and the bay. Her forefathers had been Anglican clergymen who'd arrived from Grenada, and there'd been a long line of English men and women who'd planted this land and in time became part of it. So this bay area had been part of her inheritance, her fortune, her responsibility, her world, her place of rapture—sometimes—and the stone round her neck. She'd grown up hearing many folktales of the land and the waters around here. The story of a mermaid who had been caught was just such a tale. People had been drinking; drunk men could see anything. As she turned down the jetty, holding the head of a blue marlin in one hand, she saw the young American man was still hanging around.

Hank's second shock was that, leaving aside the short hair and the mean-looking 'don't you dare' eyes and the large expanse of freckles, Miss Rain was almost pretty. Hank Clayson thought that if she hadn't stayed here in Black Conch, she might have been quite attractive. The sun had ruined her skin, of course. The decidedly strange environment had spoiled her temperament and her language was altogether backwards. It was her mouth, too. It was full-lipped and broad, like the mouth of an African. Hank Clayson had expected the overseer would be male and European. Instead, he had to deal with this abrupt, speckle-faced woman who spoke like everyone else. He felt the strangeness of the village descend on him again, as if everyone knew something he didn't. They all behaved the same way, silent and absent. His only hope was to report the mermaid catch to her. He tagged behind her as she left the jetty.

"Miss," he drawled. "Miss Rain." But he struggled to keep up. For a short woman, she walked fast.

"I have to get back to Reginald," she said.

"Reginald?"

"My son. He's in the jeep."

Hank Clayson didn't care about any son. He pursued her down the jetty, then the foreshore road.

"I need to tell you . . . about what happened. Yesterday . . ." But wind caught up in his throat as he tried to say what he had to. "I mean last night. No, I mean yesterday."

He noticed that Miss Rain seemed to nod or make some kind of small facial gesture to every single person she passed. It looked like some kind of code. Men, women, everyone nodded back. One or two said, "Morning, miss."

"Look," Miss Rain said, "I don't have much time."

She was walking on, with no intention of waiting for him.

They were nearing the depot. She put the marlin head on the stone counter and gave the men who were hosing it down a knowing look. It was still early in the morning. The village was only just coming to life.

"Give that to whoever it belong to."

"Look," Hank said, his voice cracking. "Stop. Please stop. For one moment." It was as if the mermaid, his Helen, was slipping away, as if she hadn't happened. He fought to keep himself from seizing her by the wrists, but her face was set so sternly, he didn't dare.

"Okay, Mr. . . ."

"Clayson. Hank. Call me Hank."

"Okay, Hank, what the hell happen here, yesterday?"

He stopped dead, took off his safari hat, and composed himself.

"We caught a mermaid."

Miss Rain greeted the news with a studied blankness.

Hank Clayson felt the nerves in his neck jump. He wanted to cry, throw himself at her, say that his father had gone crazy, even that he hoped his father might die out there, in the deep, the bastard that he was. They had caught a mermaid. By accident.

Miss Rain's face was placid. This was foreign man mamaguy. A boldfaced lie. Arnold was lying too, or making up one set of bullshit. American fishermen. They came and went; they snapped plenty photographs of pirogues, of sunsets, of rasta men liming, one leg cocked up against a wall; they fished and fucked the local women, smoked the local weed, drank the local babash; and now and then they claimed to catch all sort of things: whales, great white sharks, double-billed marlin, and even a merman once, some time ago. Some old colonial-times man had made up that story—Dutch, English, French, no one knew.

"Okay," she said.

Hank Clayson began to gabble and recount the story as best he could, up to the last time he saw her, hanging upside down, gagged and bound, naked, helpless. And still alive.

Miss Rain listened and nodded, all the time watching her son in the jeep.

When he was finished, she looked at him square, rubbing the marlin-head fishiness off on her skirt.

"Let me tell you something, Hank." And she looked at him cold. "You see, it's very well known here in Black Conch, especially in these parts, that we have mermen in the sea. Okay?"

Hank Clayson nodded.

"But these are all stories."

"Oh."

"Mermen do not exist. Okay? And neither do merMAIDS. They don't exist. They are stories. Old-time stories. Left over

from long ago. You know—fairy tales. Maybe you caught something. Cool. But, please . . . whatever you caught, it's gone. It's
not here anymore. I suggest you forget it all. Have a rum for
breakfast. Your father already gone back out there . . . you know?"

Hank stared, disbelieving, at her disbelief.

"But . . ."

Miss Rain gave him a look that said *no, it's over now.* She smiled
stiffly, nodded and walked away to her son, Reginald, her half-
brown, deaf son who had been waiting patiently all this time.

———

Those women figure it easy to get rid of me
Seal up my sex inside a tail
Good joke to seal up that part of me men like

The old woman was kind to me though
She was already exiled for being old
Her name was Guanayoa
Goddess Jagua transform us into new beings
turtle and mermaid
we both disappeared same night
from the island shaped like a lizard

David my one true love
must be dead too or so I figure
because he never came to meet me one year
and the year after that
when I come to Black Conch waters
on the currents with the leatherbacks
with my friend Guanayoa
Five years I went to meet him and he never came

I find a pencil floating from a boat
that was smashed on some rocks
I find paper in that wreckage
Long time events pass now
and yet I can still remember it all

———

The old man, Thomas Clayson, had spent a second day at sea. He'd taken a rifle with him, this time, and some marine flares in case they got into trouble, also an axe and a cutlass as backup to the gun. He would shoot her if need be; that would be the end of it. He'd shot big game before. He'd shot a lion in South Africa, once. The head had been stuffed and mounted and was now above his desk in his den at home. He'd shot a buffalo in the Yukon, a female too; he'd even shot a grizzly bear, once, up in the Rockies. He would shoot the bitch, no messing, bring her in. No beers on the jetty; he'd take her straight, by truck, to the other end of the island, to the port at English Town, where she would be tagged and photographed and packed on ice and taken to the larger island. There, she would be airlifted back to Florida. This time, he knew what he was up against; a big, bad motherfucker of a mermaid. He paid his crew double. He was furious over the theft of his catch, with the incompetence of the villagers, and mostly with his weak-minded sissy of a son.

But the day had proved difficult. It was overcast, the clouds low and grey and threatening to burst, and this kept the heat packed down onto the sea. Clayson had to be doused several times with ice water. The new captain wasn't as efficient or as experienced as the one they called Nicer and the crew were just a bunch of sullen boys. Clayson felt alone and abandoned on his own goddamn boat. This was nothing like the trip he'd imagined they were going to have, when he would bond with his son, teach him a thing or two about life, nature, even women, when they got drunk. He was scared the boy might not like women. As the day moved on with no sighting of the creature, he felt alone, isolated and rejected, cursing the mermaid, wishing he'd never set eyes on her. He spent the day scanning the horizon and chewing on the butt of his cigar and cursing the sea around the north of Black Conch island.

When Thomas Clayson arrived back at the jetty in St. Constance, he was badly sunburnt. His son was nowhere to be found. The foreshore was quiet. Other fishermen had brought in fish— tarpon and a large black-tipped shark. Men looked at him with unreadable eyes. What were they thinking? That he was stupid? That he'd caught something big and lost it? That he had in some way broken a code of conduct around here? It was hard to fathom the other fishermen from round these parts or read the locals, goddamn them, an illiterate, shut-down bunch of yokels. He strode into Ce-Ce's and ordered a double rum on the rocks. Ce-Ce didn't usually serve at the bar, but this time she did, with a quiet studiousness she reserved for occasions like this, when white people had insulted her staff or were about to.

Clayson wanted to argue, but Ce-Ce's demeanour said *don't you even dare*. He drowned his face in the glass and asked for another rum. He swallowed that back, too. The bar was Sunday evening quiet. None of the other men approached him or wanted to, it seemed. In the end, he said to Ce-Ce, "Who's the boss here?" Ce-Ce gave him a shit-eating look which said *you are talking to her*, and everyone knew that. Truth was Ce-Ce and Miss Rain were related; they were cousins, four times removed, and they ran the village together. Ce-Ce ran the bay and Miss

Rain ran the hill; anything that went on down in the village went through both, or one of them, but mostly Ce-Ce, because Miss Rain mostly wanted to be left alone.

"Try up so." Ce-Ce smirked, pointing up the hill. "Look for Miss Arcadia Rain."

And so, in the dimming light, Thomas Clayson marched up the steep, twisting Black Conch hill. He was sober by the time he reached her gate and the plaque on the stone pillar that read Temperance House. Small mongrels barked at him from behind the grille and ran zigzagging across the long driveway to greet him. He let himself in and they came cowering to him, wriggling their bodies for stroking, but he ignored one and kicked the other, saying, "Go away," sternly, showing who was the alpha. The dogs responded by trotting happily after him; they were well fed and loved by Reggie; they were pets, had never been guard dogs.

It was the albino peacock, perched high up on the verandah, that stopped Clayson in his tracks. A chill ran through him; was he seeing a ghost? First a mermaid and now this ghoulish bird. If he'd had his rifle with him, he would have shot it dead. The thing regarded him with righteous disdain, as he stood there in the dim glow of the porch light, in his khaki shorts and rubber fishing boots. It honked a warning to its mistress, two or three long, loud, hoarse honks, which brought her out onto the porch.

She was smoking a cigarette and had on a thin dressing gown. There was a slim, green, hard-backed book in her other hand. The house was stupendously grand; its walls were pale in the dimming light and it looked as if the roof had been trimmed with lace, which dangled from the eaves, from the porticos, from the corners of the balconies. Bougainvillea poured in riotous streams of cerise and vermilion from the porch. There was a circular driveway in front of the house with a monstrous tree that hung like a cloud over it. When he looked to the right, he saw that the garden had been cut into the hill and it went down in steps towards a cliff. A row of skinny palms waved at the sea from the cliff edge.

"Jesus, Lord," she said, annoyed, just at the sight of the old American. "I done already tell your son to go away. Now you? You gonna come up here with the same mermaid story, or what?"

Clayson was momentarily felled. The peacock started to fan and shake its long rear feathers, like it was going to show its behind. The peacock was the guard dog, it seemed. All of a sudden, Thomas Clayson felt stricken by the strangeness of it all. Miss Rain in her night garments, the quiet, elderly splendour of her home up here on the hill. He was dumbstruck, for a few moments, just like a boy, by her sturdy and yet feminine presence. It reminded him of another woman, maybe his mother, yes, maybe her, when he was a young boy and he'd gone to her for comfort. He suddenly felt put upon or caught out. He felt sorry and sad, and also tired. If this Miss Arcadia Rain was the boss of the village, then he'd got it wrong. He didn't need or want to talk to her. She was a woman. Maybe even a nice one, if a little peculiar, but a reader, with a book in her hand, just like his son.

Thomas Clayson took off his hat.

Miss Rain could have shot him dead she was so annoyed he'd come up here without an invitation.

"So. What's the story?" she demanded.

"We caught a mermaid, yesterday." He tried to sound blunt, officious, but sounded weak.

"So I heard."

"It was stolen from us."

"By who?"

"I don't know. That's why I'm here."

"So, who you figure thief this mermaid from you and your son?"

"Maybe someone living here, someone in the village?"

Miss Rain snorted. She wanted to pelt the damn book at his head, except it was a first edition of Derek Walcott's *In a Green Night*.

"Look. No man around here hiding no damn friggin mermaid in his home. Okay?"

Thomas Clayson stood his ground. He wanted the mermaid back. If not millions, and an auction to a museum, he wanted the bloody thing stuffed and mounted on his wall. He had caught her fair and square. He had papers, a licence to keep what he'd caught.

The peacock, of its own accord, launched itself into the air, a puffy cloud of white and talons. It flapped and screeched and honked and heaved its enormous wings and managed to lift itself off its perch and into the air, aiming itself at the man on the driveway.

Thomas Clayson ducked. He stood up again, angry and a bit scared.

"You're on my land," said Miss Arcadia Rain. "Get off."

Thomas Clayson jammed his hat back on. He could smell peacock chaff in his hair.

"All of it. Get off. Go. I want you and your son gone in the morning. You are no longer welcome." And with that she turned back towards the house to make a phone call to Ce-Ce, to tell her to make sure the American men left, by sea, *bon voyage*, at dawn— which they did, the old man complaining bitterly that the sea around the northern tip of Black Conch was cursed, and that the people of St. Constance were backward, suspicious and stupid.

David Baptiste's journal April 2015

Three days she stayed in that tub, watching me. I began to think it was a bad idea to try and save her. She start to change back, quite quick, maybe even from the time she was first captured, or strung up on that jetty. Something start to happen to her. She began to reverse, and then I understand she was not one of God's half-designs. She was something else. The mermaid was coming back to woman, and a woman from another time. I didn't know how long ago, but long. She had markings on her shoulders. Tattoos. They looked like spirals, and the spirals looked like the moon and the sun. I guessed she was a woman from the tribes that lived in these islands when everything was still a garden. I saw her enormous silver tail begin to come apart. It looked very old and dark. I was scared it might fall off, the end part, at least. She watch me for three days straight. I try everything to make her feel safe. My dog Harvey helped me, too. Normally, he didn't like anyone but me. He should have been jealous of her; instead, he seem to know she need guarding. He sat and watched over her day and night. They watch each other like they were talking.

The hook remained stuck in her throat, but she wouldn't let me near her face. Bad look in her eyes. Her top half of scaly sharkskin was peeling off in thin sheets. It was like she was emerging from hiding, like those mummies in Egypt. I could tell she was scared, that she didn't know what was happening. I think she wasn't expecting this changing back. She wouldn't eat. I try everything: shrimp, fish heads, lettuce. Nothing. Her eyes leaked all the time. Fishing line trailed from her mouth. I thought I'd made a big mistake. By then I couldn't put her back into the sea, not in that condition, and I wondered what I could do with her now she was there in my house. At night, she moaned, a long mournful sound, like someone dying a lonely death. In the day, she sat still in the tub and watched me. I try everything I can think of. I hosed her down, I put more salt in the tub. I try singing to her, with my guitar. She really didn't like that. This time, she don't want no music. No sweetman with no dreads singing hymns for her. None of that.

Then, one day, I was eating a small fig banana and I ketch her watching me hard. She was interested, for the first time.

I offered it towards her. She stared at it.

I went close and say, "Here you are, dou dou. Sweet fresh fig for you, my lady."

She took it from my hand and she bite into it careful, to avoid hurting her throat. She was watching me while she eat the whole damn thing. Then she wiped her mouth with her hands. She watched me again. I picked up the whole hand of fig bananas and I kneel by the tub and break off one and give it to her. She took that too. She peeled it and ate it. I could see the hook stuck up in her throat, the piece of line dangling from the corner of her mouth. But she would not let me touch her face. I wondered what she was thinking, how she was coping. How could I help this half-and-half, for that was what she was. I could see she used to be a woman, and this was what was coming back. Her hands were the first to change; the webbing fell off in clumps, like grey-pink Jell-O, to the floor. I cleaned it up. Her hands, underneath, were brown and dainty-like. I thought she must be coming back to her old self.

After that success, I try more fruit. It was mango season, so I bring her a pile of starch mangoes from the neighbour's yard, and these she eat up in one go. She liked sapodilla, too. And I fed her half a watermelon in thick slices. Soon, around the tub, there was a litter of fruit skins and pieces of her old self.

The nest of sargassum seaweed in her hair began to fall off in clumps and underneath was long, black and knotted dreads. Her ears dripped seawater and small sea insects climbed out. Her nostrils bled all kind of molluscs and tiny crabs. She'd been a home to all kinda small sea creatures, and they were slowly, over days, abandoning her, moving out. Small piles appeared by the side of the tub and these piles were active. Crabs scuttled away, sideways. I had to shoo away the neighbour's cat which came sniffing around.

I gave her water, too, every day, lots of it from the tap, in a jug. She drink that back, greedy for fresh water. It was like a game of 'test and try,' to see what she might like. I know her throat would soon go bad, infected, if the hook wasn't removed. But still I couldn't get near her. Who in hell was she? What was her name, or did she even have a name? Who had she been and where had she come from? I wondered if she would run away, the minute she could. Or try to swim home, this time as a woman.

One day, I woke up early and found her tail on the floor. It was off, completely. Large and ragged and smelling not too good. I looked at her and she looked at me and I swear I saw that she was upset and maybe even miserable to lose it. Like when snakes shed their skin. She was shedding herself, or the part of herself that was fish. I put her fish tail in a black garbage bag and put the bag in the trash can at the back of the house, wrap up well so the cats couldn't get at it.

After that, I kept watch. The dorsal came off next, the spikes on her back had been dissolving. They came off the next day, all in a row, like a long spine from the back of a dinosaur, all in one—her sail. It had begun to rot and turn gelatinous.

Seven days after I rescue her from the jetty, she look very different. Still not a human word, not more than her night moans and once or twice I heard what sound like a snore, light and snuffling, while she was asleep. Still that big hook stick up in her throat. Her feet and legs were showing, but they were still stuck together in one long, hard lump. I kept feeding her fruit and filled the tub with water. I knew this was not easy for her. When I rescued her from that jetty, it was instinct that guided me. I thought I would put a fish back into the sea. Next thing, I have a young woman coming to come, sitting in a bathtub, and she was eating and breathing and sleeping. Only then I saw better the tattoos on her body, like none I'd ever seen before: fish, birds, and signs like stars in the heavens; they were thick and look like they'd been drawn by hand with charcoal.

I kept my jalousies open and my door and other windows shut. I kept myself to myself during those early days. The American men had long gone; Miss Rain, I think, tell them to leave. People in the village forget about the mermaid within a week or so. Few had actually seen her and those who did were drunk. No one was prepared to talk too much about the subject. It was a strange time. I cooked for myself, but I noticed the smells of frying onions and garlic didn't agree with her. I ate at my small table away from her, rice and peas with fried plantain and provisions. I lost my appetite for fish. I couldn't eat nothing like that ever again—nor since. She watched me all the time. And I watched her, too. It was like our affair start, even then; so many times we just sit and stare at each other in wonder. Maybe it was attraction at first sight from that time off Murder Bay, when she first rise up from the waves. I do not know, man. Not even now, when I write this down, long time after. She bewitch me good and true.

Another day, calm so, I put a chair next to the tub and I pointed to the hook and nod my head. It had to come out.

She put her hands to her throat and looked at me with eyes

so serious and sad I found it hard to keep her gaze. I nodded my head in reply to her quiet outrage. I had to touch her. Her teeth were small and sharp; to put my hand inside her mouth looked dangerous. Then, keeping her eyes direct, slow slow, she opened her mouth. A foul smell floated out. A strong ocean stench of salt and dead fish and all the fruit she was eating. Man, her teeth needed a good brush. Her throat was a strange, deep pinky purple. I didn't want to show her my disgust. Then she opened her mouth wide, and the bad smell grew less. She made a grunting sound and her eyes looked stern and ready. In her own way she saying *Okay, do it.*

With a small pair of pliers I dipped inside her gullet and twist at the hook. It was buried in the side of her throat. It tensed and contracted and her eyes seeped. The hook had latched on tight so the barb was poking through on the outside. It would have to be turned back. I poured rum on the outside of her neck and then, steadily, I tugged. I watched her, saying, "Okay, dou dou, okay. Hold tight." Her hands were grasping the side of the tub. This was the first time I came so close to her. She was half-naked in the tub and I was without a shirt. Our bodies were young. Even then, I think, she and I, we yearned for each other. From those first hours, even then it was in the air, this trust that grew in time between us. I tugged at the hook with great care and it slipped out, eventually. Some blood flowed from the outside and the inside of her throat. Her face was calm but not grateful when I showed her the hook.

"See?"

She made a screw-face and glared at me. I didn't know her story, yet. I didn't know why she came to be like this. A woman had been living inside a fish. A miracle. Now she was turning back. I didn't know how lonely she was, not then. I knew nothing of her past. I dressed the puncture wound on her neck. It look like she get savaged by a vampire bat, not a boat full of fishermen. In my head I cursed the Americans for what they did. Her wound started to heal within a day or two, as did the wound from the gaff hook, and her shedding continued. I did the best I could to clean up the debris around the tub. She shed her old fish suit in clusters of scales that looked like rusty silver coins. I noticed the same spirals on her breasts. I was aroused. She had a young girl's breasts, ripe and pointed, and all of a sudden I had a hunch as to what happen to her. I offered her one of my old T-shirts to cover her nakedness. She didn't want it. I guessed that she come from a time before clothes. Was she something the past had left behind? I didn't know how or why. She stared at everything like she seemed to be reading everything: the air, the shadows, the floor, the light. She gazed up at the wooden ceiling with curiosity in her face and this made my insides swim with happiness. She craned her neck to see out the windows. Stern and quiet, she watched me smoke my cigarettes, like she know about smoke. I thought her people must once have lived an ital life and I learn in time she was greeting it all back. She saw meaning in every natural thing that lived. She was saying 'hello' again. I left the T-shirt on a chair. Eventually, she accepted it with a nod.

———

Days pass in tub of water
drinking it and it taste bad
Not enough salt
My tail rotting and it happen quick quick
Old legs seeing them again
But I am a cursed creature

Back on Land

Women jealous jealous of my young self
Put me in the sea
a thousand cycles ago
I am cursed creature
cursed to be unhappy
What happen to me then?
Fish scales fall away
Breasts like young again
I come back to woman
My new old self start coming back
I was woman again and I was frighten bad

Man watch me good
David who rescue me
Sea mami he call me
mami wata
Long time I did not walk on land

One day my tail fell on the floor
all in one piece a big part of me
How would I swim away?
Now even the kingdom of the sea is dying
filled up with plastic

I come from red people
good people
I was in the south
where Kwaib people also lived
people who kill and make war
Red people were my people
all killed from disease

and by the murderer admiral
Miss Rain tell me about
when I came back to being a woman

———

Miss Rain had been writing in her diary, which was her daily custom. It was her son's tenth birthday the following week. How would they celebrate? Soon she'd be sending him off to camp in America, and there he'd meet, for the first time, other deaf children of his own age. Reggie, named after his great-great-grandfather, liked to write his name in full: Reginald Horatio Baptiste Rain. For now, Reggie's world was marvellous but small. Peacocks and small, loyal dogs, her massive library of books, and of course reggae music because the low-pitched bassline was so loud, felt almost more than heard. Reggie was in love with the music of Bob Marley and Toots and the Maytals, because he could feel the bass. She'd bought him headphones because he wanted to play the music so loud it scared the peacocks. It was common to see Reggie dancing near the record player in the large wooden-floored ballroom, listening to reggae.

They'd both learnt American Sign Language from a tutor from California, Geraldine Pike, who had been hired on and off for the first six years of Reggie's life. She was a hippie and a poet and had given Reggie pride and self-esteem; she had told him about the deaf community out there in the world. She had introduced him to deaf poetry and stories with hand signs; she had released him, very young, into the riot of his full potential. He could read books, write words as well as talk with his hands. He danced, made up his hand poems and constructed sculptures from found objects in the garden or house. He knew that he would be a Black Conch poet one way or the other, using sign language and words. He knew he would one day go away, leave St. Constance, just like his father had—for more or less the same reason. He would live a good life; that much he had already planned.

Life, Arcadia's only-time partner, knew about Reggie but had more or less fled before his birth. His departure had been a shock and then a more lasting devastation she did her best to cover up. Had one of her brothers warned him off? Had there been a way for them to live as parents here in this house? She loved it too much; she hated it too. She'd told Life she could never leave the house, but then she figured he'd simply had enough of the picong and the talk of 'house nigger' in the village, the consequence of loving the white lady up on the hill, lovers since childhood. As Life had grown into a man, their love affair stumbled. He wasn't happy, and she couldn't please him as she had when they were youths. He wanted more than Black Conch, and he minded that she was rich. They argued a lot. Her parents didn't approve. There'd been two pregnancies, which had both ended in miscarriage. But then a third pregnancy stuck, Reggie.

But Life done leave her ass, and his own boy chile too. He had made his point, and it had been a punishment. She had come down with measles and Reggie had been born deaf. She had thought herself still young when Life departed. Now she was older, a decade of her mature adulthood lived solitary and confined in her castle on the hill, living with her humiliation, the horned woman with the luxury of a cliff-top view. No one felt an inch of pain for she, in her faded peeling house and the acres of forest that went with it. Waiting and then not waiting. Her sadness had changed her into another woman altogether; it had wearied her and it had also blossomed her.

David Baptiste's journal, April 2015

Around day ten, her legs started to come apart. One long stump separated into two. She stared in wonder at her new legs—in fact her old legs. I was still careful around her. One problem was shit. She began to shit the fruit she eat and this floated in the tub. We both knew she had to come out. So, like with the hook, I made the first move. I offered her my outstretched arms but she refused to come. "Please, dou dou, I go hose you down," I said.

But she didn't understand. She only looked at me with dread, as though I was going to hurt her, just like the American men. Still no words, just squeaks. I worried we had come to some kind of end of things. But there was the practical problem to solve; how to get her out of the tub?

She tried hoisting herself on her arms, and then tried to make her legs work, but they wouldn't. It was messy and awkward. My old T-shirt was covered in shit and she pulled it off. Somehow, she struggled and slipped, then clambered naked from the tub. I help to heave her out and then she was on the floor, in a puddle, crouched down on her knees, hiding herself with her long dreads. Quickly, I hosed her down, saying, "Okay, honey, okay, now, doh worry, doh frighten." Then I covered her in a big old towel. She didn't move at first, just hunkered down, hiding.

She ent no longer what she was, that was for sure. She was scared, like being unlocked from a prison and given freedom. I was scared too, of her and for her and what to do next. The situation was not like anything I knew about. I hadn't tried to capture a woman, let alone planned to hide or look after a woman. So, I was always on the back foot. Something new happened every day. If I left her for too long I was fraid of what go happen next, of what new change might need my attention.

She couldn't use her legs. They were still soft as soap, and so, careful careful, I towelled her dry and wrapped her up and carried her upstairs, to the room where I slept. My bed was just a double mattress on pallets, but it was comfortable and dry and I was ready to let her share it with me. But that was a joke. She ent having me share anything so close. Quickly, I got the idea she remember what a bed was. She actually snarled at me and gave me such a menacing look I backed away. She ent want me to share no bed. I watched her cover herself with the towel. I found her some of my clothes too, an old jersey and a track pants, and I threw them to her and she looked at me like she understand to cover sheself. She needed covering now, no more sharkskin suit or fishtail to hide who she was. Yes, a young woman in my bed now; and not no friendly woman at all, none of that. I went back downstairs and started to cook myself a simple meal. I heard grunts coming from upstairs. I wondered then if she go try to run away. And though I wanted to help her, for a time, if truth be told, I also wanted her to go. I was afraid of what I'd brought into my home. I knew she was from ancient times, from times when people knew magic, when people saw gods everywhere and talked to the plants, the animals and even the fish in the sea.

I ent check on her till early morning time, and when I did, I found her fast asleep, wearing my old clothes, curl-up under the sheets like a child in the womb.

———

I climb outta dat tub one day
I wonder if the curse was gone now
I could not walk
Legs soft soft
David give me clothes to cover my body

I did not want them
My people did not wear clothes
He gave me his bed
I woulda kill him if he come near me
I did not leave that bed for many days
I had not sleep for long long time
And so I fell asleep
I dream of my sisters
I dream my mother
I sleep and sleep and dream of long ago
I feel like I was in my dream
What was real?
What was dream?

4

Legs

≈≈≈

THE RAINS CAME HARD IN MAY THAT YEAR—early, for the rainy season. Every time the rain came down, it sounded like thousands of gloved hands clapping. The daily downpour was a mixed blessing. With the rain, every man and woman felt an old, lingering, hard-to-dissolve guilt for past sins. The rain brought awkward memories and nourishment, together.

Every morning, the mermaid, Aycayia, half-slept and listened to the rain, and remembered more and more of what it was to be a woman. She enjoyed the sound of the rain's soft heaviness. It reminded her of her old self, of long ago, when she had lived in a village on the island shaped like a lizard, when she was the daughter of one of the wives of a brave casike, when she had six sisters. She tried to remember the name and then the face of every man who'd visited her, and watched her dance; then she tried to forget them all again. Her loneliness echoed in her bones, the centuries swimming in the sea, half-fish. She wondered what had happened to the old crone she'd arrived with—Guanayoa. After the huracan, Guanayoa, a wise old woman who told uncomfortable truths, had been cursed too, changed into a leatherback turtle, and that was how she'd ended up so far away from the coastline she knew. She had followed Guanayoa's instincts of migration. As she lay under the thin sheets of David's bed she wondered how and why she'd transformed back into a woman. She wriggled her old toes, which were now her new toes. She curled herself into a C and listened to the musical sound of rain on galvanise and felt comforted because she knew that parts of the world hadn't changed. There was still rain. This meant there were still clouds, sky, birds—a world she could read.

The bald earth drank up all the rain. The tough white grass turned green. Mornings were cool and hazy. Mist clung to the tops of the mountains, where the temperature was cool. Large, matronly macajuel snakes, heavy with eggs, unfurled themselves and travelled slow slow through the dense rain forest, seeking the crystal water that gathered in pools in the creviced roots of trees.

The rain trapped David inside. He didn't go out to fish. *Simplicity* was anchored in the bay and filling up with water. He would have to go and bail it out some time soon, cover it with a tarp.

The mermaid, who'd turned back into a woman, had spent three days in his bed. He'd slept downstairs, on a pallet, on a piece of foam. It was okay, but he was deeply troubled by his new inhabitant. He dreamt of rivers and caves, he dreamt of his father, Leonardo Baptiste, who'd disappeared with his uncle, Christophe Life Baptiste, long ago, to the larger island and he wondered how they now lived, wondered if they ever looked back and thought of St. Constance. Both of them had wanted more than a fisherman's existence. Black Conch was too small and so they had disappeared, and few had heard from them since. The Black Power revolution had happened over in Port Isabella, and the prime minister had long ago said 'Massa day done' and yet little had changed in Black Conch since then. Same old. Miss

Rain and her family would never die out completely; the Rains and the Baptistes were all cousins here, anyway. White families still owned land like they used to and black men like him came and went, looking for the promised freedom of independent living. Besides, coming and going was the way of all these islands. Come and go. Mix up, move on. Leave seeds behind in the form of human life, outside children. Most men he knew had many children; his grandfather Darcus Baptiste had produced fifty-two. David had lost count of all of his siblings and halfs. David's father and uncle were long gone, though many of his other uncles and aunts were still around, like Ce-Ce. His father had left him the pirogue, a livelihood at least.

And then this mermaid woman. In his bed, mute, just squeaks and grunts and snores. Long matted hair, covered in tattoos and she didn't like to wear clothes. She had started to eat some starch—corn and sweet potato, all raw, as if she knew what they were. She ate what he brought and she pissed and defecated into a small covered pail in the corner. She was very young, topmost twenty years old, and unique to behold. It was her eyes—they were silvery in the whites, and they gazed at him with such fierceness and, in time, such gentleness, it was hard to endure her gaze. He felt those looks she gave him came from a different time of human consciousness. Her eyes scrutinised his soul. Who are you, they wanted to know. Her hands were still strange, with the remnants of webbing. Her ears had been pierced and hung a little. Everything about her was a mystery and suggested antiquity. Her skin was red-brown, like people from the Amazon. Excepting Guyana and Puerto Rico, he knew her people were mostly all gone from the Caribbean—except in tiny pockets and mixed in with other groups. Did she know? Still, not a word in any language.

Then, one morning, a surprise. She appeared, on hands and knees, behind him; she had crawled from the bed, down the narrow stairs. David jumped backwards when he saw her, kneeling, looking up at him through her long dreadlocks. Her face was hopeful. She tried to raise herself to her feet, but it was clear her legs were still too weak.

"Ayyyy," he said, in greeting and relief. He wanted her to get accustomed to him.

She didn't speak, not even then. She watched him, as she had been watching him for days. Then she raised up her hands towards him, for help.

"Come, nuh." Hand in hand, then her forearms balancing on his, they spent the morning walking together, crippled and awkward and slow, her legs bending in all the wrong places, as she moved in zigzags across the room. One foot, then two, toe-to-heel, in front of each other. It wasn't easy, but at last David began to feel comfortable being with her. She was coming to come, as they say, coming to come back to who she once was. And who was she? A princess of noble lineage, or just a common girl, like anyone else? Mother or virgin (with those pointy breasts)? What knowledge did she have that he had never known? He could only marvel. One thing was clear: she had travelled forward in time; she was young and she was ancient. The year 1976 was a time of big change in the New World. In the papers he'd read about women's struggle in the university and marches for power to black people, so she'd arrived at a good time, if any, to come back.

David Baptiste's journal, April 2015

I spend all that morning helping her around. She walked all left and right, like a newborn baby tripping over her own legs and feet. She have she legs trap inside a tail for so long, they were useless. But she didn't want to give up, though she seemed scared to be back on land and who could blame her. This island ent the same island she was born to. But she wanted to walk again. I got the idea that there was some place she might go to straight away, once she could walk, that she might try to run to. All morning I held her up, by the arms, while she tried to stand and walk across the room. I figure she could use a frame to walk, like the kind old people use. Next day, I made her a frame from old pieces of wood. After that, she was at it every day, putting one foot in front the next. She needed the exercise to build back the muscles she'd lost; she needed to increase her strength and then, once she did, maybe her legs would remember themselves back. When I first saw her, off the rocks of Murder Bay, it was like she was walking on moko jumbie stilts, but that was her tail keeping her upright. That felt like a long time ago, since I see her head pop from the waves, but it was only weeks. Next thing, she was living by me, sleeping in my bed, learning to walk, and I was in stupidy about her.

In truth, I was a captive man from that first morning when I was singing hymns to she. I can say that now, many years later. She rise up from the waves and watch me, and when I look back into her face, I knew I looking back into the past of these islands, and into my own history as a man; my own damn self she was showing me. She had come to claim me and teach me about the giving of my heart as well as my loins, of being more whole than I'd been till then. I was enraptured by her and also afraid, because she ent become no mermaid by no accident.

Then, one day, maybe two, three weeks after I rescued her, there was a knock at the door. It opened before I could say come in. Aycayia was sitting at the table, with a plate of slice-up Julie

mango and grated sweet potato. She seemed to have some memory of what it was safe to eat raw—yam she would not touch.
When the knock came, she jump off the chair at the sound. My
neighbour, Priscilla, walk in, cool so, in time to see a young red
woman in my jersey and track pants crawl on hands and knees
across the room, fast fast, and up the stairs.

I was damn vex with Priscilla for marching in. Priscilla was
the meanest woman in the village, in the whole of northern Black
Conch, maybe even in the whole island on account of her bad-
mindedness and petty behaviour. And she just happen to live
only five houses up on the other side of the road. Priscilla had on
a short pants and high-heel sandals with her black bra poking out
from she vest—cut down at the neck to expose even more of her
breasts. Priscilla was pure malice, always on about how much she
hate Miss Rain and her stupid deaf-dumb bobolee son. Priscilla
try to run me down many times in the past; she was always in
my tail for sexing and I never liked she at all; too damn vex all
the time. She had big buckteeth like a rat, yet she figure she was
hotness self. I ent have no time for she and yet she like to chase
me down. She is why I keep so quiet when the mermaid arrive,
all my doors closed.

Priscilla was furious and surprised all in one go at the sight
of my new friend.

"Eh, eh!" she exclaimed. "Since when you have a woman living here?"

"Since when is okay for you to come barging in?"

She give me a look, straight. "I knock, you ent hear?"

"You hear me say come in?"

"Who de ass that woman up dere?"

"Who de ass you feel you is to aks me?"

"What wrong with her legs?"

"Priscilla, I'm busy. Why you come here?"

She looked around the place and spied the walking frame I'd built for Aycayia.

"She's a cousin," I say.

She give me a look upwards to my bedroom where Aycayia was hiding. "Seems so."

"So why you here?"

But nothing get past Priscilla.

"She have fonny eyes, too. Where she come from?"

"Jamaica."

"Oh, well Miss Jamaica have fonny, cokey eyes and she cyan walk. She Syrian?"

"Some people have a disability, okay? She staying by me for a while. Now why you here?"

"Nuttin. I just ent see you around lately."

Priscilla give a big sexual smile and stare me down. It made my blood freeze. "Why you so vexed with me, chunkaloonks?"

That was it. "Priscilla, get out mih damn house now, okay?"

"Ayyyyy! Mind you manners."

"No, you mind yours. I'm busy. I have a visitor. Go away. This ent no parlour for you to drop in anytime."

I open the door and say, firmly, "Goodbye."

She look upwards at the bedroom and then she fix me with a look I know to be her baddest look of all, and it say, *I ent done with this yet.*

"Okay," Priscilla say. "Good afternoon."

That wasn't a good sign. Priscilla was the mother of Short Leg and Nicholas, both of them on *Dauntless* when they ketch her. I hear both of them boys scared no ass by the mermaid and I worry bad what they going to do if they find she had change back into a woman and she was living so close by. All of this concerned me since I'd been hiding her. Not just Priscilla. How was I going to keep this new 'lady friend' quiet, eh? How long could she stay with me before people get to know of her? People in Black Conch were too suspicious, *oui*, and I know Priscilla had a thing with Porthos John, the superintendent in the next village of Small Rock. At least one of her children, Short Leg, was his chile. If she told Porthos about the mermaid, then what? I ent want no ten-foot policeman in my house. Not with this mermaid woman, so innocent, and lovely.

———

Exile = to stay away from home
Exile = to be rejected from home
Outcast, cast out
My life was exile from home

I meet Bob Marley music in Black Conch
Get Up Stand Up Duppy Conqueror
Bob Marley was half white
he was half and half too
Half black half white ghost
Mix up good like me
I learn from Reggie
He tell me that Bob Marley
love a white woman
and hate his white father
Bob Marley is half and half
Reggie is half and half
He have white mother
and he half and half too
None of them half fish

I danced alone on the cliff
live in house with old woman Guanayoa
Men still come
husbands come to watch me
I live quiet quiet in small home with an old woman
Women say I make their men into slaves
take away their freedom of will
Men cannot stop themselves from loving me
I was pretty pretty
Women put curse on me
me and the old woman
become mermaid and ugly old turtle
I still young
lonely like Reggie
No one to talk to
I lived in the kingdom of the sea for long long time
World of silence
but they talk down there in their own way
Radar speaking says Reggie
and so I learn a new way to talk
My old octopus friend I miss her
I never saw her again
For many years I live with fish
Did not know how many centuries pass
I see canoas get very big engines loud loud
I stay away from them
I see people in canoas who wear clothes
I figure to keep far away
The kingdom of the sea is big big and it have own ways
And so the life of a mermaid is the life of a visitor
I watch and keep to myself

Stay away from the lion fish
Stay away from big big sharks

Aycayia is my name from long time ago
Sweet Voice
I fraid of man but I fraid women worse

———

Days after the appearance and ejection of Priscilla, Aycayia was
practising walking again. In the afternoons she shuffled along
with her wooden frame. If David watched her, she would ignore
him. Head averted, she kept up her slow plodding gait, sometimes in small circles. Often she ended up on the floor, panting,
on her knees. She wanted to walk again, but the ocean, after
centuries, had destroyed her legs. It wasn't just walking she tried.
Singing came next. Humming to herself. In bed, at night, when
David lay downstairs, she would hum her sad laments for her
sisters and for the island shaped like a lizard. Her voice was coming back, too, and it sounded like the ocean, though still not yet
strong.

David slept badly. Often he woke up hard as wood, yearning
for the mermaid, though she was a puzzle beyond understanding. First she was half fish and now she was almost all woman.
She was a legend that had come to life. Maybe fishermen had
seen her and her kind, here and there, in the vast oceans, over
centuries and maybe those stories were based in fact. When she
wasn't being wary and suspicious, he sensed a quietness about
her, an attitude of gentle kindness—to his dog, for instance.
She'd changed his comprehension of what it was to be human.
She had appeared in March, from the waves, half-naked, her

true nature hidden, her story unknown, no name. She had swum so long in the sea, she had forgotten how to speak the words of her people, Taino, the good people. He'd read about them in a book they had at school—about the first people who came to the archipelago. She'd stolen his life away. She'd inflamed his heart and mesmerised his senses. At night he dreamt of her dancing on the cliffs of a neighbouring island in the archipelago. The sky was green and the yellow sun bled into the blood-orange sea. In these dreams, she emerged from the reddish earth and offered him handfuls of mud. His loins ached with longing. An intuition pestered him that they had met before, that he'd even been searching for her, out there, by those jagged rocks off Murder Bay. She looked twenty and yet she was also very old; she seemed sweet natured, an innocent, and yet she had swum the oceans alone, endured an eternal exile.

Three weeks in, she could demolish platefuls of raw cabbage and sweet potato. A mango she ate whole, skin and all; the stone she sucked bald. She still shuffled along on her frame. Her feet were enormous and bunioned; her toes were webbed. The arches had collapsed and so her feet caved inwards. She still didn't like to wear clothes. Sometimes she forgot and walked around naked and David was fearful for her if she stepped outside into the yard with her pointy breasts and tattoos. Her long black hair, knotted into dreadlocks, grew more and more matted. She still smelled like the ocean, a strong sea salt scent. David remembered more of the history he'd learnt in school about her people and the Spanish conquistadors and feared he might kill her with everyday germs.

Then, one night, he heard her voice. There were no words, but what he heard sounded like a soprano singer practising scales. Up and down, and then long solemn, rich melodic sounds.

She had the sonorous voice of a much older woman. She sang down deep into his bones, a slow song of remembrance. David climbed the stairs and found her sitting upright in his bed, in the moonlight, her eyes closed, singing to herself. Sensing him, she opened her eyes but continued. For the first time she did not seem frightened of him. He began to wonder if her song was about something that had happened long ago, about why she had come to be in the sea. Whatever, it came from the heart. She let him watch. When she was finished, he went closer and sat down on the bed, not too close, for she still gave him a stern face.

"Song," he said to her.

She nodded, understanding.

Next day, in the pale great house dripping with lace, when the rain had stopped and the afternoon had stilled, Arcadia and Reggie sat down to mathematics, to the mystical Greek formulas of circles, such as pi × r squared. Reggie had been homeschooled by Arcadia and Geraldine Pike from early on—who still kept in touch by letter. After she realised Reggie was deaf, Arcadia had thrown herself into researching what was best for him and she'd found out about sign language and schools for the deaf, but these were all in America, and at that time there was nothing suitable, even on the larger island. She paid a vast sum to lure Geraldine to Black Conch and Geraldine had saved Reggie from social exclusion by giving him language and, even more, ideas.

Reggie was now trilingual—American Sign Language; Black Conch English, which he lip-read; and Standard English for books. He was a proud child. He didn't want to wear a hearing aid, none of that trying like hell to fit into the hearing world when he was so permanently different. He wanted to be himself, a group of one, a tiny minority of just him. With his headphones on he could hear the bassline of Bob and Toots and Aswad, and that was enough for now; besides, he reasoned, those musicians would all end up deaf one day too.

Reggie signed that he hated Pythagoras and asked who he was and if he had been a very clever python.

Arcadia signed, No, Pythagoras was a math genius. He understood circles.

Reggie signed, I do too. Would you care to study my formulas?

Arcadia signed, Probably not, or not yet, and okay, no more school, for now. We will continue with this tomorrow. Time to visit Uncle David.

Reggie signed, Cool.

When Arcadia and Reggie Rain knocked on David's door they waited. Aycayia had time to hide upstairs, but David was close to despair. By then, he'd shared his home with the ex-mermaid for nearly four weeks. He was smitten, but she was messy. She was slovenly, in fact; she'd not only ejected him from his own bedroom, but littered it with half-eaten mangoes and fruit skins. He had to empty her pail every day. And while it had been hard, at first, to get her to wear clothes, when she finally accepted them, it was hard to convince her to change them. She inspired awe, but she smelled bad. She sang in bed every night and he'd begun to fear his neighbours would hear and get nosey. Slowly, slowly all the walking practice had paid off. She could stand without the frame. Soon, she would be walking. Then what? Where would she go, and how could he begin to explain her existence to his neighbours, let alone the village? He'd gotten used to the way she looked, but he wasn't sure if she really passed for human. It was her eyes, mostly, they were too bright.

"Hello," shouted Arcadia.

David opened the door.

"Hello, Miss Rain," he whispered.

She glared at him.

"David, what the hell happen to you?"

David was taken aback; apart from Priscilla and the ex-mermaid he'd seen no one for weeks.

"How yuh mean?"

"You look like shit. This place stink. What happen?"

"Nuttin."

Miss Rain steupsed, rolled her eyes and walked in. Reggie followed her. He was wearing a Burning Spear T-shirt and mirrored sunglasses. He looked like he was in a reggae band already. He bumped fists with David.

"Serious, man," Arcadia said. "What happen?"

She drew up one of the two white plastic chairs and looked around. "It smell funny in here, and your pirogue go sink soon if you don't go and empty it. What's going on?"

"I been quiet, miss, das it. Minding myself and doing chores."

Reggie was looking around for objects to make things with. It made David nervous.

"Let me fix you some tea," David said.

"Okay."

"Anyway, ah come fer a reason."

David filled the kettle with water, struck a match for the gas burner and held it till a violet flower danced.

"I come to ask you about your uncle."

"Oh, who, which one?"

"Doh give me that. You know damn well and good which one."

When he turned around he saw she was actually blushing, which he'd never seen before. Miss Rain wasn't the blushy type. She looked young, more like thirty, though she was ten years older than that. Her life was well known and also mysterious. She kept to herself but everyone knew what had happened. She get horned real bad. His uncle Life was a sweetman and a horner-man, well and true. Reggie had half-brothers in Black Conch, for sure, but no one had yet put together who they were.

"Is Reggie's tenth birthday soon," she began.

David nodded.

"I figure he deserve a party or something so. I been think-ing . . . you know."

David nodded again but he was also watching Reggie.

"I figure we could invite a few people round. Maybe. Like you and . . . Ce-Ce . . . and you know . . ." She was looking a little anxious. "I even wonder if . . ."

The kettle shrilled. He took it off the hob with a mitt.

"Oh gosh, nuh man, damn and hell, David, you know what I mean."

"No, miss."

She looked at him straight. Her eyes were a little wet. "You ever hear from or see your uncle Life?"

He looked at her, wishing it was different; she wasn't a bad woman. She was way too good for Life. He left her good and proper, for a sexy high-class town brown woman in Port Isabella. That much he did know, but he would never say such a thing to her. She didn't need to know that.

"No, miss. I ent ever hear from him. Or my father. No one hear from them long time. They in Port Isabella."

"Nothing?"

"No." It was a small lie. He'd heard Life had an exhibition not too long ago, that he had started hanging with the arty crowd in town. He wasn't too interested in Life or his father to be honest.

"Miss Rain," he said, "Life ent coming back any time soon, I reckon."

She nodded. "Yeah, I figure that too. I just want Reggie . . ." And they both looked towards where Reggie had been standing, but he was gone.

A shriek erupted from upstairs.

David froze.

"What the hell was that?" asked Miss Rain.

David quailed and closed his eyes.

"Oh Lord, what's that child doing up there?" Arcadia leapt up and ran up the stairs.

David stayed downstairs, helpless. At least it was Miss Rain.

"David, Daviddd, come up here NOW."

Aycayia was sitting up in bed, in his dirty jersey and track pants, with her matted dreads, her eyes shining bright like stars. Kneeling close to her was Reggie and he was signing to her and she was nodding and trying to copy him. Miss Rain was watching them.

David came up and saw the mermaid and Reggie busy with their hands, saw Miss Rain's wonderment.

"Who the hell is she?" asked Miss Rain.

"I can explain."

"David, she doh look normal."

David bit his mouth and nodded.

"She have strange eyes and hands, you know. Who is she?"

"She's the mermaid, miss."

Miss Rain turned to look at him. "What?"

"She's the mermaid them white men catch, three, four weeks ago."

"David, please, don't tell me this." She put her hands over her ears.

"Miss, is true, I cut her down, rescue her. Is me who thief her."

Arcadia stared at her son, who was giving the mermaid his own language.

"David, no."

"Yes, miss."

She shook her head and tears welled.

"Them damn stupid Yankee men came to tell me all about it. One almost get his head buss by one of my peacocks. No."

David nodded. "Yes."

Arcadia stared hard. "Shit, man, David."

Tears fell down David's face, hot, salty; he was relieved and he'd been scared, not to say tired. He hadn't slept well at all these last few weeks. It all welled up.

"What in frig's name happened to her?"

"Her tail fell off."

"I can see that."

"Yes. It all fall off. She start to come back almost at once."

"Oh." Miss Rain was shaking her head.

"I figure I was gonna take her back, as a fish, put she into the sea. Instead, she start to change back . . ."

"Oh. My. Word."

"She only now learning to walk."

"Oh."

"I love her, Miss Rain."

Arcadia gasped.

"Yes, it happen instant like."

"Shit."

They both stared in awe at the mermaid and the child sitting on the bed, making hand signs.

———

First few days with legs I sing of the sea and loneliness
Then I meet Reggie
Miss Rain shocked when she first see me
she shouted NO like she see something terrible
Reggie make talking with his hands
That is how we meet together
with our hand language
Language of the time before time
When Reggie left and Miss Rain left
I lie flat in bed
I sure they go come back
Then what?
I start to sing to myself
David come and watch me singing
Just like olden day time, long ago
Men like to watch me

One night I go watch David sleeping in his bed
Quiet quiet I go close to him
I watch him long time
alone with sleeping man
I watch his nose
I watch his closed eyes
Watch his body go up and down with breathing
Up down like the sea
Like waves inside him rolling up and down

I watch David like I watch orca whale
Feeling outside life

I am a watching mermaid
always watching to keep safe
I watch him sleeping a long time
Asleep he look like a boy
Was he my enemy too?
Feelings come I did not understand
One night I watch him whole night

———

David Baptiste's journal, May 2015

After Miss Rain came and she see the mermaid that first time, we sat downstairs and talked for a long time. Reggie stayed upstairs, but me and Miss Rain talk real good for an hour or more. Miss Rain smoke cigarettes back to back as she talked. She wanted to tell me about Life, about how they know each other as children, how she loved him from then, twenty years and more, from when they first set eyes on each other. It give me a shiver because it was the same for me with Aycayia. Life was her 'heart-mate,' Miss Rain say, and this raise the pores on my skin and I feel bad even thinking of the idea of a heart-mate.

I surprise to hear Miss Rain talk so openly. I feel sad for her too, because I figure Life never really trust himself with her, like she too big and white people hoity-toity up there in that house. I always figure Life didn't leave she; he run away to big himself up, because he feel small. 'House nigga,' I used to hear people say. No one believe in how he could be with her, live in an equal way. I figure Life wanted to be equal to Miss Rain up there on the hill. I figure that's why he left, not just her, but Black Conch. He was an artist too, and wanted to make himself known. But Miss Rain saw it different. She just feel sad and sorry. She miss him bad; they were loving each other since children, or so she said that day. Both of them were barefoot country people as children. Miss Rain never saw the bigger picture. She cool, don't get me wrong, eh? But she don't know the other side of things, of how black men live; specially a man like Life with talent, who wanted more for himself. Miss Rain ent see any of that; she just feel bad bad in her heart and missed him, like she didn't care who he wasn't. I told her Life went away to make a man of himself and she tell me he already was a man in her eyes. He don't need to make himself better, she said. She loved him, and Reggie had never known him. Reggie have talent too, like his father. Reggie always wanted to meet his father. That day, I feel sad sad for her and the boy.

Next thing, Reggie came down with a big smile on his face.

He and Miss Rain made one set of hand movements and then Miss Rain said Reggie invite the woman upstairs to his birthday party.

I stared at Miss Rain.

The two of them watch me. I ask if Reggie knew she was a mermaid.

Miss Rain signed the question and Reggie nodded yes.

I look at Miss Rain and her son and feel good, all of a sudden. People could make the best of a bad situation, sometimes. Reggie was a cool little breddren. He not stupid, like Priscilla said. He wasn't dumb at all; he just deaf.

Reggie made hand signs to me and Miss Rain interpret them. He asked me to come for lunch next Sunday, me and the fish lady. He explained there would be music. I told him okay and Reggie watch me and laugh.

"Like the mermaid a real hit, boy," I said.

Miss Rain rolled her eyes and ask me if I think the mermaid-woman could live here, in Black Conch, in this house with me. I tell her I ent know, that I was making it up as I go along. She ask about the neighbours, Priscilla and them, and I tell her Priscilla already see her.

"You watch that bitch," Miss Rain say. "Cause she could cause you real trouble when she ready."

I tell her I know that, and that Short Leg and her other son see her and they were on the boat. Nicer had hired them.

"Shit," she say. "That Priscilla have a mouth like hell, and worse than that. She bad like bad self and she don't like me."

I nodded and Miss Rain steupsed and looked upwards. Then she asked if the woman was deaf. I said no, and she say I could teach her language just like Reggie did. I ask how, and she explained she have teaching books at her house. ABC, all kind of thing. She taught Reggie to read and write, and is not so hard and she would lend me some.

That made me feel brighter, and the two of we stayed like that for a few moments. Both of us know I have quite a thing going on upstairs. Reggie seem to understand that too.

Miss Rain said 'okay,' like she make some kind of decision, then she say she gone and she will see me in a few days.

Reggie came and hug me up and I choked back a sudden fit of tabanca about the mermaid, about him, about just about everything.

"Okay, breds," I say, and hug him back.

I sat down at my table after they leave and figure my life change big time. I ent know how exactly, not then. All I knew was that everything was different; life use to be simple, easy. Now it was the opposite. Women make life so, and that is why I never share my house with a woman before. And she was messy, boy, and all that singing at night. I told myself I would ask her to have a bath. I had to get back my position as owner of the house. She had moved in and she gain control, without a word. I needed my house back. Even Harvey liked her. Funny that, eh? Local pot hound, guard dog, fisherman's dog, first mate, territorial as hell, bark at anyone who come within a foot of the yard, seemed to find she a natural housemate. She had put obeah on him, or what? How does a man accept a woman, any woman, into his house? Just like that, let alone a mermaid. Life changed quick, boy. I never plan it so. Later I saw that change came as change always comes, from a chain of events with a long history, too long to see from back to front, till it come.

Next day, rain was pelting down hard, like the sky had opened its mouth and was letting everything out. It fell hard hard on the galvanised roof, and yet this seemed to make Aycayia happy. She grinned at David, standing there in the centre of the room, hanging on to the walking frame, and he was surprised at this sign of recognition. She'd loosened up since Reggie had come over, even eaten a boiled potato. Around them shutters flew closed and banged open again. Next thing, Aycayia let go of the frame and pushed it away. David was bolting back a shutter, when she shrieked out a sound like a bat or a bird. He turned to see her, mouth set, eyes pinned to the floor, making one big-footed step forward, unaided. He almost went to help her, but her face said no. One big footstep forward and she fixed him with a wicked grin as if to say *okay now*. But she was stuck there, without the frame. Next thing she lifted up her back foot, like a space astronaut, picked it up and placed it on the floor in front of her first foot. Then she looked up, her eyes glistening, and her face broke open into a smile.

David almost fainted at that smile. He stood there, stupidly, watching as she kept it up, this slow space-like walking, her arms like wings stabilising her. All she needed was a helmet and space boots. Aycayia hadn't walked for centuries; even so, she still had the memory of walking and for a whole day she stopped and started, balancing with her arms. One big foot, then two. When she got tired she would sit down on a chair and stare at the floor.

At midday, David fixed her a plate of raw bodi and pumpkin. She smiled at him again. He almost fainted a second time. Woman messy but easy to please after all, he figured. He watched her big feet; she needed shoes, walking in sneakers might make her more stable. He had some old Adidas sneakers she could try and he went to find them in his truck. When he came back, she was munching the pumpkin skin. He held up the shoes and pointed and she signalled she understood.

David stooped by her feet and took one and jammed it into one of the sneakers. It went in okay. He looked with renewed wonder at her feet. Webbed toes, no doubt about it.

"Okay, push," he said to her. Her hands were balanced on his back. She laughed a little and David felt his body tense and he dared not look back at her, because this was new: a laugh? When the shoe was on, he tied the laces and looked up at her young face. She nodded, serious. He managed the same with the next foot and sneaker, avoiding looking too closely at her webby toes, tying the laces tightly. Aycayia wasn't shy at all about her feet. So, in 1976, her first shoes were a beat-up pair of old, green suede Adidas with three white stripes. He let himself hope that here, at the northern end of Black Conch island, she had a better chance of survival than in other places on earth, and maybe even a chance of blending in.

When the sneakers were on, she stood up. Her chin jutted as she took a step forward. This time, it was better. The size nine Adidas had rubber soles and gave her more grip. Off she went again, one foot, then the second. The awkward space-hopping stopped. She concentrated on taking smaller steps. It worked, though it was some time before she got the hang of it. David watched while she walked diagonally across the room many times, slow slow, her arms coming in closer. It made him consider how much he took for granted; he couldn't remember learning to walk; it was just one of those things every child does. Watching her was like watching a small miracle, a butterfly emerging from its sleeping bag of a pupa, or a baby duck planting its webbed feet down one in front of the other. He wondered briefly about his own first steps, and who'd been there to catch him when he fell.

Aycayia spent the next three days practising in those old sneakers. Like the clothes, once on, she refused to take them off; she even slept in them. She still wouldn't let him near his bed. It was hers, now. He suspected she was hiding things under the sheets; there were lumps here and there. Was she still shedding? Then it came to him he should bring the bathtub back in and fill it up with the hose. It was his own damn house, after all. Had his willpower disappeared entirely since she'd arrived? One afternoon he went upstairs and gave her a look which said she needed to come down. When she saw the bath she seemed resigned. She began to take off the stink clothes and stood there, naked, in front of him, her tattooed breasts covered by her locks, her hands covering her pubis. She got in, one leg at a time, the sneakers still on, and she lay down low in the tub watching him. He went and found a piece of soap and handed it to her. She didn't know what it was, so he showed her. Then he left her alone to bathe and wash herself and he thanked the Lord, for what, he knew not, maybe just because she could walk and would soon be clean again, like a normal woman.

Later, when she was wearing fresh clothes, a next tracksuit bottoms and T-shirt, he handed her a toothbrush. She stared at it, shook her head, not understanding what it was. He demonstrated with the brush and his own teeth and she laughed again.

Tears welled in his eyes. Three laughs in one day. Something had changed. He wanted to keep her safe, always. But he also suspected that wasn't what she necessarily wanted or needed. In fact, now she had the sneakers, he expected her to disappear someday, just like she'd appeared. One morning she would be gone, leaving behind her mango skins in his bed and taking his heart with her. 'Heart-mate.' He didn't like those words. He handed her the toothbrush and pointed to a basin of salted water on the table. She scrubbed her teeth with the toothbrush and gargled with a glass of water. He put the kettle on to make some bush tea to quell his stomach, a fire of nerves since Miss Rain had come with her son. A birthday party? With music? He had been up to her house only twice in his life, both times by specific invitation, to bring something she needed—a barrow, a lawn mower. In truth, Miss Rain was almost as hard to predict as the mermaid. If Miss Rain wanted to see you, she would appear. She came down to you, you never went up.

But now Miss Rain knew about his secret visitor; she had even told him he could teach her words, and maybe even how to read. Was it even possible that the mermaid-woman might be here to stay with him indefinitely?

And where the hell was Life? And where the hell had his father gone, too? All of a sudden, he wanted them home. How could men pick up and leave their women and children? It was Reggie's birthday. He was ten. Good piece of age on him now. David sipped from the cup of bush tea.

Aycayia was watching the setting sun. She was reading the clouds. She was gazing at the kingdom of birds. She was drinking in the world outside, a world she understood. She'd spent all the time up to now readjusting to her old form.

David's house stood amongst a nest of banana trees on the hillside. There was a small porch and then there was a bay view where you could see the sun's rise and set every day. Aycayia watched the colours in the sky and the silver dance of the sea. A tear fell.

"Sea," David said.

They watched as the sun flooded the sky with hues of ochre and violet and red. The sea looked far away and everywhere. Quietly enormous, it was a kingdom unto itself, one they both understood, where they'd come across one another. He wondered if she missed it, or whether for her it had been a purgatory. Was she relieved to be walking again as a woman, able to continue her life in the Caribbean once more? Could she start over again? She was young enough. He wanted her, but he also hoped she could be free to be whatever she wanted. She smiled at him and this time he caught a look which was quietly hopeful. He had the feeling that, for her, something was either over or just beginning.

5

Speech

≈≈≈

BLACK CONCH WAS A HELLUVA PLACE, Miss Rain often said, and the northern tip of the island was a special type of hell. Her earliest memory was of a low, incessant growl through the night, like thunder and bestial hunger mixed together, a growl that said *I'm coming to shred you,* but it was only the howler monkeys in the rain forest behind the house. The Rain land included some of the most ancient rain forest on earth. She'd grown up with this rumbling, imminent threat that one day she'd be eaten alive. If the howlers didn't get her, then a macajuel snake could slip out from the forest and coil itself around her in fat tyres and crush her in her sleep. Hell had a sound, and it was the howlers. Hell had a smell, too, and it was brought on the trade winds, the scent of the land-locking sea. Hell had shadowy ghosts, too, the souls of thousands of slaughtered Caribs and kidnapped Africans, who had once toiled on what became Rain land, and died there too.

Over four hundred years, Black Conch island changed hands twenty-three times. Settlers, buccaneers, naval men, rogue and official, arrived and departed from St. Constance for centuries.

Some were left alone by the Caribs, others were attacked and killed; some gave up, but not before naming bays and hilltops after a piece of Europe. Every bay had seen a bloody sea battle and there'd been countless murders on the beaches. White men of varying types arrived again and again, all with inflated notions of their possibilities. Usually they bit off more than they could chew and abandoned their attempts at domination and fled, deciding no, it was all too difficult. Caribs, disease, other Europeans, hurricane and drought had beaten them back. In their retreat, the Dutch left a battery of two cannons. The French left a church. The British abandoned a steamship depot. Much later, the Americans left a radar station. Even Black Beard and Captain Morgan had arrived at northern Black Conch and, it was said, left buried treasure in the hills.

Archbishop Rain, Arcadia's ancestor, had been an Anglican priest. He'd bought the land twenty-seven years after emancipation and built the house from mahogany from the forest. The stone he had shipped from England. He named the house Temperance. One hundred and sixty slaves had worked the land up to the year of emancipation. Many of the Congo men became fishermen after slavery done, but a handful stayed on what became the Rain land and eventually became tenant farmers and settled to tending land which could feed them. The Rains had been the first planters to pay their labourers. The government bought a large parcel, finally, and sold it off to villagers. It was good land, fertile as hell in this helluva place. Over the centuries, the land had been planted with nutmeg, indigo, ginger, cotton, bananas, cocoa and sugar cane. Now, the large sugar mill wheel lay at the bottom of the hill, so rusted you could cut your hand on it.

Hell had been ripped apart, too, by nature's tempests. Two massive hurricanes had swept through Black Conch, a hundred

years apart, devastating the land. The last one, in 1961, had flattened eighty percent of the crops on the island and entirely
ended the production of cocoa, by then mostly cultivated by tenant farmers. It was this hurricane that saw off Arcadia's brothers,
Archie and August; both of them done with the place and they
decamped to the larger island to find work in town, even though
they were born country men. Their children, all half-brown and
half-white, had left too.

Arcadia was what was left of the Rain family in St. Constance.
She had been more or less given the broken-down estate to run
as she pleased and she had more or less left it to the villagers. The
fish market was a co-op run by Ce-Ce and her brothers. The forest was protected by wardens from felling and poachers. Tenants
tended their own crops. She had made it easy for the villagers to
rent, buy land and build on it. Tourists had trickled in to this end
of the island, like those Yankee men the other day. Helluva place,
yes, yes, then and still, and, unlike other planters, she knew just
how big a clump of land the Rains had bitten off: 2,000 acres,
of which 1,400 remained. It was land she knew intimately, girl
to woman, land in which she had come to understand the heinous sins of the white men before her forefathers, and then
their sins, the severe barbarity of their pious Christian souls, and
the cruelty of the climate too. She had come to terms with the
strange fact of being a white woman with a Creole song in her
mouth. She knew well a certain kind of loving up in those hills,
and it had broken her into womanhood when she was just fifteen
years old, the kind of sexing that made her shudder and drip and
her heart swell open and pour itself out into this difficult world,
the kind of sexing that taught a woman to hold herself and wait.

David decided the best thing to do was back his truck into the yard in front of his house and open the door to the cab. That way, the ex-mermaid might understand they were going on a trip. They had no proper names for each other yet; secretly he addressed her with many names for sweetness and affection, and they were jammed up on his tongue: dou dou, lover, friend, hunny. She had inspired an outbreak of chivalry in his heart, something dangerous, if truth be told, should it run riot. This type of passion for a woman could ruin any man. She had caused his heart to wake up, to writhe free from its constraints of mistrust. Her radiance and her innocence showed him what he'd been longing for all his life; her strange silence had dissolved his usual aloofness with women. He was used to the St. Constance women, who knew him too well, who already had his merits and failings marked out, who liked to cuss and criticise and used more direct and earthy ways to seduce his loins. All the men knew all the women around here—in all the ways there was to know. This woman was different and everything about her threw him back on himself. It wasn't just that his blood take, no, not just that. An admiration had seized him. Her people had died out, whoever they were. Now he could see who they'd been. It was like she'd opened a door in the universe, showing him the first people who had lived long ago in these islands. His heart softened for the loneliness of this woman he'd rescued, something he'd never expected to feel for anyone.

When he showed her the truck with the cab door open she shrieked and ran back upstairs.

"Dou dou!" he exclaimed, "No, no, is okay, hunny." He followed her and saw her body like a hump under the sheets, balled up and trying hard to disappear.

"Come, nuh, dou dou. Doh frighten." He sat down on the bed

and tried hard to imagine what she must be thinking. It took him half an hour of sitting there before she peeped from the sheet. He was mystified as to how he found such patience with this woman. Everything with her took a great deal of time.

When they arrived at Miss Rain's home at three o'clock in the afternoon, Reggie ran to greet them. He'd been a little disappointed they were so late. He'd fallen for the mermaid, too. She was different, just like him. He opened the door of the truck and there was light in his face, a raw delight in his greeting. He and Aycayia walked away from the truck, across the lawn, Reggie making hand signs and jabbering away and the mermaid engrossed in his hands and what he was saying. Trust flowed between them as they walked together. The peacocks strutted in front of them, sweeping the lawn with their spangled, opulent trains. The white bird, alpha and territorial, preened itself from its position atop the garden wall.

Miss Rain watched them approach. She was standing on the porch, a hard lump in her throat. Reggie never talked like that to anyone else, not even to her.

"Thanks for coming," said Miss Rain. "We still ent eat the cake yet."

David went up the stairs to the porch, tentatively. Despite being family, he'd rarely been inside the house.

"Come in," Miss Rain beckoned, and he followed her indoors to a large room with a highly polished wooden floor, a room where people might have danced long ago. It was painted a pale lemon and it felt light in there. The wide-open windows were shielded by thin bamboo blinds and two old ceiling fans revolved silently, mixing up the air. In the centre of the room there was a circle of sofas and armchairs, arranged in a nest; one of the chairs was a curvaceous rattan rocker. Old carpets were thrown down on the floor. For such a large space, it seemed cosy. Miss Rain had made a kind of room within a room in there. But it was the wall of books that had David gazing with astonishment. Miss Rain collected and owned thousands of them. Individually, they looked sturdy; packed together tight they looked like a vast cliff face of colourful hand-painted bricks.

"Come into the kitchen," Arcadia said. "I'll put the kettle on."

The kitchen was big too. The cabinets were made of wood and had curtains against the glass. The white surfaces of laminate were curling off and chipped. There was a long wooden table in the centre and above it a gnarled tongue of glue-paper hung from the ceiling, with many flies stuck to it.

There was a cake on the table, on a cake stand. It was fluffy and green and had ten pink candles. It had been decorated with silver balls, pieces of candied fruit and sprinkles.

"Reggie decorated it," she said. "Sit down. It's just us, anyway. Ce-Ce couldn't make it. Best this way, maybe."

David pulled up a chair.

Arcadia filled the kettle and put it on the gas ring. She turned and fixed David with a faraway look, trying to focus on something that she hadn't quite worked out how to say. Life was David's uncle. David was Reggie's cousin, and yet the truth of it had somehow been denied. For some of the villagers, it was as if Life hadn't really existed, and Reggie had no actual father. Arcadia had kept quiet. So had David. This was the way of a small place full of interwoven families. From birth, people developed the necessary social skill of being duplicitous. Be polite and mind yer own business. Never say true things if it didn't help matters; in fact, the truth often made matters worse. The present was complicated enough. And history? Well that had been the tragedy that lay behind it all. The truth was often way too painful; it would end in talk of heinous crime. So no one bothered to speak of it.

Even so, now she looked at those ten candles, Arcadia wished she'd done things differently.

"David," she said. "Yuh ever wonder about yer dad?"

David's eyebrows shot up. "Not often, miss."

"Call me Arcadia, for God's sake."

He looked at her like he didn't want to.

"I mean, you ever felt close to him?"

"No."

"You figure you ever gonna have yer own chilren?"

"Sure."

"You have any yet?"

"Not that I know of, miss."

She gave him a look.

"I mean, Arcadia."

"I remember your father well, you know. Leo. Quiet, humble man. Like he was never here and yet he was always around."

"Yeah."

"You miss him?"

"No. Not really. Is not for me to miss him. Is mih mother who bring us up."

Arcadia nodded. Black Conch men roamed, women stayed home. Only time men and women came together in St. Constance was to pull the seine late in the afternoon, drink a rum or two down at Ce-Ce's, or intermingle thighs in the blue hours.

"Family is hard thing, sometimes," said David. "Too many of them to know and too many of them too different. I figure is always best to keep distant to keep family."

"My own all left long time," she said, and she thought of David's mother who had passed away two years ago; she had been a fine baker and sold bread from her kitchen window. Arcadia could almost smell Miss Lavinia's bread, as if her soul lived in the phantom scent of freshly risen yeast.

"You miss them?"

She rolled her eyes. "No. Family is tears."

The kettle whistled and she took the kettle from the hob.

A silence descended. Arcadia wanted to say more. Maybe the time had come when she could say 'enough.' Draw a line. Move on.

"Where is my son?" she asked.

David looked over his shoulder.

"Next thing go happen is those two get lost and we have to send the wardens to find them in the bush."

"Doh worry, Reggie won't wander too far."

Just then loud, mournful, soulful reggae boomed from the room next door.

"Shit, man," Miss Rain exclaimed, as reggae music thundered into their bones, into their chest cavities. David grinned.

Miss Rain raised her head, as if to catch the scent of her son There was no point shouting. The loud music said *This is how deaf I am*. They left the kitchen to see what was going on.

Dozens of vinyl records had been pulled from their sleeves and lay scattered across the floor. A peacock had flown inside and was perched on the rocker. Aycayia was standing by the record player with her eyes closed, seeming lost in reverie. Her hair hung to her backside and swayed around her in long matted ropes. She was beckoning high up into the air, making small steps across one another, pressing each foot lightly into the wooden floor, as though to make sure each time she placed her foot it left a print mark.

"What de hell," Miss Rain muttered.

Aycayia was moving in small circles, arms raised, in the room that had been made for ballroom waltzes. David, Reggie and Miss Rain watched, and felt a lurch in their stomachs, a stirring up of some hard-to-reach part of themselves, a fluttering sense that this was a ritual dance beyond their understanding.

Miss Rain turned to David and said, loudly, over the music, "Yuh know, Reggie really ent have too many friends."

David nodded.

"Not too many people could be friendly with him, anyhow."

David nodded.

"Is like she starting from scratch, again. Reggie already teaching her his own language . . ."

"Yeah."

"You know, I could teach her our language, Black Conch parlance. Like I teach Reggie."

For the first time since he'd seen this mermaid off the jagged rocks of Murder Bay, David felt he'd heard something that sounded like a sensible idea.

"If she gonna fit in, she gonna need to talk, you know."

Aycayia was dancing her lonely, soulful dance. David had already dreamt of her dancing on the cliffs of another island. She was of a different order of things. Could she fit into Black Conch? He'd always thought of the place as kind of slow and quiet, but she had shown him the opposite. Black Conch was the present and it was complicated.

"That would be a good thing for her," he agreed.

Miss Rain left the room and came back with the green cake, the pink candles lit and dancing with tiny flames. She signed to Reggie to turn the music down.

When Aycayia saw the cake, she stared with intense curiosity. "Happy birthday, Reggie," Miss Rain said aloud and signed. "Make a wish."

Reggie closed his eyes, breathed in deeply and blew all the candles out in one breath. Like his mother, he had been born upstairs in this house, and had never been anywhere but Black Conch, but now he had a sense that something had started. His life had begun at last, as he knew it would. He was ten, had come of age, with the great blessing of a fierce mother.

The four of them sat on the chairs in the nest of a circle and set to eating the fluffy, iced green cake, chocolate inside. Aycayia ate it with her webby hands, stuffing chunks and crumbs into her mouth and nodding, thoughtfully. No one said anything.

Aycayia was no longer quite so scared. She had recognised many things on this island: the smell of it, the night sounds, the type of daylight in the mornings, the type of heat at midday, the way people walked around, lightly, making no sound, the way they glanced at each other with nods of respect. Then there were the birds and the plants, the trees all around, the warm earth; all of it flooded back, her world of living gods.

Aycayia felt she could be home again and yet she knew home had dissolved in her memory. She wanted to be with these people, one of whom wasn't able to hear anything and spoke with his hands. They'd been kind to her, including the fisherman with the guitar. There was another call, though. A strong tug at her centre, in her womb, a feeling of loss, and the pull came from the sea she'd known for many centuries. She knew it was waiting, and yet she'd lost her powerful tail. What had happened? Had the women's curse dropped? Was it because those women were all now long dead? Had she done her time in exile? Then it was like another type of curse had come and for what reason she didn't know. Men had pulled her out of the sea, where she'd been safe but lonely. Now she was contending with another life, one with reggae music, peacocks, cake and people who wore clothes. And there was the way David watched her; it made her feel connected to him; it made her belly soft and gave her feelings between her legs. She put her hand there to hide these feelings and wondered about them. So long inside that tail. Now this. She ate her cake and longed for something she could not name.

David Baptiste's journal, June 2015

I felt real strange when I left Miss Rain's home. I returned back many times after that, but it take a mermaid to get me invited inside. Cousins, she and I, and yet it never really feel that way till then, even though we pass each other many times. Many things kept us separate, call it slavery times, call it what you like, but it take a mermaid for me to mingle with a my blood relative here in Black Conch island. I left feeling, well, fancy that, a mermaid does be a revolutionary. But I figured Miss Rain have she own set of complications. Is why she always remained aloof and apart. Me, I was just a hardworking fisherman, boy and man. I was schooled in St. Constance and English Town; I knew who I was and where I from. The sea gave me my livelihood. I figure then, and even now, that the sea give me my greatest lesson with Aycayia.

She fall asleep on the way back and started to snore. I like that sound. Truth is, after a few weeks, after she started to walk, it become harder to remember she as a mermaid. I only saw her as a woman. I leave her in the cab of the truck and went inside to fix up my house. 'Family is tears,' Miss Rain said, but I figure the truth is 'Woman is tears.' In what used to be my bed I found what she was hoarding: spoons, forks, rubber bands, and I even found an old conch shell she must have taken from my porch. I find other things too—a candle stub, tea bags. I changed the sheet for a clean one. I shook out the cover sheet. I swept the floor. Just as I figure it was time to take back my bed and my room, she appeared at the top of the stairs and give me a look which make me feel so sad for her. I left the room quiet quiet. "Sleep good, dou dou," I said to her.

I never knew what go happen next with her in those early days. What could I compare it with? I slept downstairs on what feel like a bed of stones. Me, a young man, restless for sexing, yearning to be up there with her in my arms, and yet nothing about her ever say 'come.' I had to cool myself, take a longer view. Not every day a man does get the chance to meet a person like she. I figure Miss Rain go teach her words to speak and Reggie would teach her his language, and then things would get better. I figure I could teach her words, too; all of us would help her in one way or another. I figure she now have friends in St. Constance. Maybe she could settle here, in truth. Small village at the end of nowhere. Why not? She have the right people on her side. I think then that she could be my wife. Crazy thing, I know, but I had that feeling right in the centre of my chest. I would marry her, if she say 'yes.' She was already in house! I figure all kinda big possibilities in those early days with Aycayia. Is easy for a man to get mix up when it comes to a woman. Lawd, we don't understand the half of them, and yet is she who teach me what woman is and a man should be.

I slept feeling better in myself than for weeks. I sleep and dream of the ocean and of Black Conch island long before man live there. No humans at all; no Adam and Evelyn or Bible story. I dream of a quiet place, natural like, and I dream of an island

Speech

where no man—red, brown or black—did live, of Black Conch before it have any human footprint on it. It have only garden and nothing to spoil it. No man own it or cultivate it. Not yet.

I woke up to the sound of the sea washing in the new day. I felt quiet quiet in my soul. Upstairs Aycayia was snoring. I made myself some tea, and say to myself I will see what happen next. My boat needed tending, so I went down and see to it. For the first time in weeks, I left Aycayia alone, walked down into the village, home for my whole life, and yet everything feel different and people even watch me different. People say "hello" and yet they watch me like they know something had come to pass.

———

Part of me still alone
I am back on land and yet a stranger to this island
I cannot use language
Boy teach me his language first
and I learn quick quick to use my hands to talk
Boy is my first friend in Black Conch
David is a man
Different set of situations

I figure Guanayoa still in the ocean waiting
I lived with her too before huracan came
and the waves took us out to sea
What if a next huracan come?
I take the big shell from David's porch
to call to her one night
let her know I'm alive
Nobody but her know who I am
I was human again, trying to learn quick

I was not sure if this was my dreams come true
I was lonely I missed the sea
I missed my loneliness
I was trying to understand everything
Heart mixed up
The man David make me feel mixed up

———

Every afternoon, around three o'clock, David dropped Aycayia to Miss Rain's for lessons. There, at the table in the grand room with wooden floors, sat an indigenous woman of the Caribbean, cursed to be a mermaid by her own sisterhood, whose people had all but died out, slaughtered by the Castilian admiral and his kind; a woman who, as a mermaid, was pulled out of the sea by Yankee men who wanted to auction her off and if not that, stuff her and keep her as a trophy; a woman who was rescued by a Black Conch fisherman; a mermaid who had come back to live as a woman of the Caribbean again. She sat quietly puzzled as she learnt language again, from another woman she wasn't sure if she could trust. This woman was white, dappled with freckles, and no matter what she wasn't, she was of the type who had wiped her people out.

Arcadia was self-conscious because she only spoke Black Conch English, a mixture of words from the oppressor and the oppressed. This parlance was the language she was teaching Aycayia, as well as written standard English.

They sat for many hours in those early weeks, both tentative and aloofly marvelling at each other and their task. Outside, the rainy season arrived in full and poured itself down in sheets of silver. The peacocks honked and now and then strutted into the house. The pot hounds lay curled under the table. The howlers could be heard too, grunting in the forest. Quiet quiet, for hours, they sat together learning the alphabet, the structure of an English sentence and words like table, chair, apple. Miss Rain noticed Aycayia had another way of forming sentences, and she guessed that she once had another way of arranging words and it was still there, in her knowing.

Reggie came and went; his school lessons were in the mornings. Now and then he gave Aycayia his headphones so she could hear the mighty Bob singing "Slave Driver." It was a quiet time, June and July 1976. Not much happens in Black Conch in those months. Rain comes down heavy. Everybody who had seen the mermaid on the jetty back in April had forgotten her long time; she had dissolved into local lore.

Aycayia drank in the new languages she was being given, American Sign Language, Black Conch parlance and the type of English written in books. She soaked it all up like a sea sponge; she had been so long dry in her mouth for language, thirsty for conversation. Slow slow, it all began to come together. One day she looked up from her books and gave Miss Rain a hard glare and said: "I dance to want." Her face glowed.

"Good," said Miss Rain. "Good start."

After that, new words multiplied and more jumbled sentences flew from her mouth and every time it was a surprise and every time it made Miss Rain and Aycayia a little more secure in their association. Her own words began to loosen themselves, too. When she reached for the jug she remembered its name, *jiguera*, and then what was inside, *toa*. Miss Rain nodded, hopeful that Aycayia's lost language could be recalled.

And still her eyes were very bright in the whites and still her hands and feet were frilled with a tender, rose-quartz pinkish webbing. Still she walked with a listing gait; still she watched everything and everyone with an open and gentle expression. She would sink into reverie, her face poised upwards, as though watching something somewhere else. She gazed towards the sea, often. She still had that strong salt-sea aroma. Dressed in David's track pants and T-shirts, his size-nine Adidas sneakers, she was ancient and modern, an indigenous woman and becoming a Black Conch Creole. The tattoos on her shoulders told of a people who had a sacred connection to birds and fish, moons and stars. Her face shone. She was 'coming to come' as they say in Black Conch. In time who knew what might happen, if she could 'pass' again as human.

Then, during that same morning when David had gone to tend his boat, Aycayia was alone in the house when she caught sight of Priscilla through the window. She ducked down, but Priscilla had seen her. Aycayia stood shivering with fright, her back to the wall, trying hard to stay quiet. She could smell the ammonia of urine as a warm trickle ran down her thigh. She wanted to go back to the sea kingdom to hide, to be alone again, without other women. She stood still for several minutes. Then she popped her head back to peep out; Priscilla was still standing there, looking in. They stood, face to face, just a wall and an open window between them.

"Who de hell are you?" Priscilla said.

This Aycayia understood. She didn't reply, but slammed the window shutter in Priscilla's face and hid again, against the wall, breathing quickly.

Priscilla poked the shutter back open again with a stick.

"Eh, eh," she said, righteously. "Cousin? Das who you is? Eh? Miss Cokey-eye? Cousin, like hell. Come, nuh."

Aycayia wouldn't move from her spot.

"Ayyy, I know you in there. I just want to meet yer. Eh, lady? . . . Lady with the fonny eyes."

Aycayia trembled. Was it happening again, already? How long had she been in Black Conch? Weeks, not even a couple of months? She took a deep breath and went back to the window.

They stood eye to eye. Aycayia decided she would clobber this woman hard if she tried to come inside. Though she came from a people who practised peace, there was a time for self-defence, and there had been warriors in her tribe. Her mother had been a warrior, a casike's wife. She would slap Priscilla's face if she had to.

"I here," she said through the window, and her voice was soft-strong. She had been famous for her sweet voice. But those words, to Priscilla, sounded foreign, her accent hard to fathom.

Priscilla scrutinised her hard and Aycayia let her look, but when she was done looking, Aycayia opened her mouth and let out a blood-curling growl from centuries long past.

Priscilla backed off, like she see jumbie in this woman's silvery eyes. Aycayia gave her a look which said *stay away from me.*

Priscilla stumbled away, muttering her bad-minded thoughts. What manner of woman was David preferring to her after all this time as neighbours? A madwoman? Or was she retarded? Why was he hiding her away? No one else heard the commotion but Priscilla went away scheming. She was born vexed, or so people said.

David had a square piece of mirror downstairs in his house that he used to groom himself. Aycayia had avoided it till then. After she was sure Priscilla had left, she decided to look into it. The sea never gave her much of a looking glass, so she approached it with trepidation. She peered into it for several minutes. Her eyes bled tears; it was a shock to see herself. She hadn't aged at all, not since she was last a woman. And yet she wasn't the same, not the same girl at all, the one with six sisters, all drowned, the one who'd been happy once, but only for a short time. She saw a version of her younger self, saw that her long and lonely life in the sea had left its mark in her eyes. She gazed for a long time, trying to remember the days before her banishment. The suitors who'd pursued her were now a blur, each face merging into one. She hadn't given herself to any of them. Some had wanted her as a second wife, or even a third. One tried to bribe her father with land, another had promised her a new house of her own. She had held fast; she had been too sad about the death of her sisters. But still those men arrived, ardent, insistent she choose one of them, offering her everything. And still she had danced. She hadn't understood her power over them and the resentment of the other women. Then the big huracan had appeared from nowhere, ferocious in its wrath, bringing with it her centuries of exile. Aycayia gazed into her young, old, sad face, greeting herself back, saying one new word again and again, slowly, as if to cast a spell: home.

David Baptiste's journal, June 2015

Early, early, before dawn, I took my pirogue out to sea, to the same rocks off Murder Bay. The water quiet, and a small bit of rain coming down. Is like my place to go and pray. I drop anchor and sit for a while. I ent really go out to fish. The sea dark and the sky still dark too. There ent no feeling quite like being alone in a boat in the night. Land in sight, *oui*. Out there ghosts visit on the breeze, they visit from centuries past, from a time before all of we get mix up and lost. Though I always know who I was in Black Conch, family history don't go back far. That memory was rubbed out because of the badness of slavery. Baptiste is plantation owner name, French man name from way back. Yuh think I happy with that? I figure my real name would never be known to me, a mystery. I felt myself fill up with pain, with ol'-time loss from those days. It does come from nowhere now and then. The feeling come like a message on the wind, or that is how it ketch me. Now and then. Mostly, when I was out alone in my boat. That is where I met my soul friend, the mermaid woman from so long ago she cyan remember sheself either. We were both lost people. I felt all twist-up in my chest, sitting there in my boat. Was that feeling for she or for us both?

I knew that ghosts came onto the land from the sea. You could feel them out there. I sat and wondered just what kinda men get murder here in this bay and for what reason? White men arrive from far away and then sail back to where they come from. I always figure is feelings of being insecure that make someone want to take from others. The white men who came here were full of jumbie spirit, always restless. Ghosts come into the bay, ghosts of white men, and red men and black men like me, and these ghosts come like a current bringing unease and nervousness. Is only my humble opinion. But this is what white men bring here to the Caribbean: trouble. Then and now, they always looking, then taking something.

Dawn arrived slow and gentle. I looked around and saw something in the water up ahead. I ketch a feeling of dread in the pit of my belly, like another woman go raise her head from the waves. Last thing I need. Just then, I saw a big leatherback turtle break for the surface. She made her way towards me, swimming slow. No other living creature in sight, just me and that old leatherback and is like she heading straight towards my boat. I stand up and watch her come; she covered in moss, like she have a piece of land on she back, and is then the thought come from nowhere that she have something to do with the mermaid. I rev the engine quick, for I ent want to get possessed again. I pull up the anchor and get outta there fast fast and leave the turtle there, big so, covered in barnacles. I figure she know my boat engine too. No, man, strange times. I headed home just as the sun rise and the other fishermen were heading out. I wondered what else was out there in the goddamn sea for men to catch.

———

Miss Rain teach me the language of Black Conch island
She say it was a type of English parlance
She teach me like she teach Reggie
her own son born with no language
so we had that in common
I had forgotten mine
thousands year old language
vanished from my mouth
Miss Rain tell me her son born deaf
when she catch measles

Weeks pass learning words like give and take
like peacock like jamette and mamaguy
like all of what these things mean
Speech is freedom
I begin to speak as much as possible
Couldn't shut me up say Miss Rain
I ask her many questions
How is your house made?

Speech

With wood and cement
Who is the chief here the casike?
She told me I am
Miss Rain is not a casika
She tell me her family own
a part of Black Conch island,
but that is not the same thing that casika means
Miss Rain teach me plenty things
and new words too

son of a bitch
in a nutshell
table
chair
heart
wajang

I ask why everybody in Black Conch is black-skinned
She told me how black people came
I ask her where are the red people like me
She told me they were mostly all dead and gone, murdered
I learn from Miss Rain
how the Castilian admiral
MURDER all my people in a very short time
My people long dead
I sobbed
She told me many black people were murdered too
I ask if the Spanish Christians own everything now
She said not anymore and turn red in her face
like the whole thing happen in a short time
only five hundred years when the world is very old

This all happen quickly
My family own all of this part of the island she say
Land is not to be owned I tell her
Strong pull all the time away from land back to the sea
but I never want to go back there
I want to stay my woman self
even here when my people long dead
I want to be here on land again
but deep inside I know there is still some mix-up
I am still half and half
half woman and half cursed woman
cursed still in this new place
Same same all over the place
The sea is a strong pull
but I want to stay human

NEW WORDS:
chennette
dance
dog
cake
because
broken
love
family
mango chow
good night

6

The Fish Rain

AT NIGHT, AYCAYIA COULDN'T SLEEP. A future with the possibility of possibilities kept her awake. A deep sense of knowing had awoken in her from long ago. It had to do with being a woman and all that being a woman meant, of living as a woman.

She lay upstairs in David's bed, with one hand on her heart and the other on her womb. For centuries she'd travelled the cold waters of the ocean, searching for the possibility of a mate. But there was no coupling with her own kind; not one merman had appeared in all that time. She touched herself down there and wondered about David. She had been watching him, watching him watch her. The feeling down there, between her legs, was powerful, like a force of its own. It had been keeping her awake at night and she knew it had to do with him. The fisherman smelled good, a man smell, a skin smell, a home smell, his body warm. As she lay in his bed she could hear him breathing loudly downstairs. It was dark outside. She hummed a quiet song about her sisters. They had all been older than her, all of them fair of face. They had all kinds of secrets—she knew that—and they had kept them from her, the youngest, as if these were secrets she would understand later, when she was a woman, old enough to be married. But she'd had many dreams about marriage, and in those dreams marriage always turned out to involve her death. She'd never liked the idea at all. Instead, she had danced and sung her songs. Aycayia, 'sweet voice' was a name she lived up to. She attracted men, couldn't keep them away, but hadn't accepted any of them. She didn't want to be married: a wedding would kill a part of her, so she'd not accepted any man. Then her six sisters had drowned, in an accident in a canoa, and she'd been left alone. The men had pursued her still and made their offerings to her father. But her father was too stricken with grief to let her go, his last daughter, and so she had escaped.

The ache between her legs felt bigger than her, than her fears of marriage and death, and it flowed up from her lower half of its own accord. It sent a hotness through her up to her heart, made her feel awkward and full of tension. She tossed and turned, not understanding what this ache was, why it had come on her, and was so demanding. Maybe this ache had been present in her loins for some time, maybe since she'd first seen David in Murder Bay. Had she started to change back to being a woman even then? A fisherman. He'd lit her up and she had stayed close to the Black Conch coastline because of him, distracted, her insides aching. Maybe she'd carried an ache with her all these centuries. Then she'd been caught, yanked from the sea. She listened to David's heavy breathing, and felt terror over her thoughts about him, of his hands, his secret parts. Oh! And yet she also wondered what it might be like to lie down next to him.

Quietly, she rose from the bed and crept down the stairs. A hurricane lamp lit the room so that it wasn't pitch black, but full of shadows. David was asleep in the corner; he was lying there, one arm raised above his head, the other fallen to one side.

Aycayia approached, fearful, but also compelled to look at him. His chest was rising up and down with his breath. She went close and knelt down. There was a thin cover over him that had slipped. He was naked except for a pair of yellow jockey shorts. She had the feeling that if he woke up, it would be the end of her, the end of something, or that it might even be the start of her life as a woman. He would reach out and take her in his arms. She could sense this feeling between them, that he knew about it too, and that it wasn't something they could keep on ignoring. How she had wanted to be with a man and how she had feared men. She watched his chest rise and fall. She watched his smooth smooth skin, man skin, black like squid ink, black like the darkest sea, a silkiness stretched over him. She studied his forearms and his hands—strong, strong. On his chest there was a smattering of what looked like tufts of grass, short, fuzz-like. She wanted to touch it but dared not. His face was quiet, his eyes fallen shut, like he was at peace; his breathing was deep, not snoring, just deep and loud, and this made her smile. What was he dreaming about? He was dreaming good and strong, for sure.

She wanted to lie down next to him and fold herself into his body. Her sisters had withheld secrets and she wished she knew them now. What to do? What to give to a man? How to be with one? Miss Rain had said 'man' was called many other names: father, son, boy, lover. Lover was a sweet thing, Miss Rain had said, and her face was sad. She, Aycayia, had been cursed, sealed off inside a heavy tail, banished to waters where there were no other creatures akin to her. There she was no longer a risk to the other women in the village. Her sisters were no longer able to show her anything. She would have to cope by herself.

She watched David's face long and hard. She wanted to kiss him on the lips. She wanted to hold him by the hand. Soon, she knew it would be their fate. She saw the smooth long form in his jockey shorts and felt this was the strongest part of him, and it too was asleep. It was the part of him she was most drawn to and most wanted to look at—and it was also the part of him she dreaded. It was life and death. It would be like a long sword which could kill her off. It was the secret all full women knew about. She would have to face it, that long thing, the secret part of him, like a snake in the woods of his thighs. It was designed, she guessed, to give him and her pleasure. But, also, it was designed to kill her off, lead to her maiden-death. Yet it was the part of him she most wanted to explore, those hidden parts of him, the hills and slopes down there. She and him, were they going to be just like the dolphins she'd noticed in the ocean, locked together, in a dance, riding each other? She knew it was about a way of coming together. That was how things worked.

Aycayia gazed at David till dawn, till her knees ached and till she needed to sleep. She felt all kinds of things for this man: soon, soon, it would happen. She held her belly as she gazed at him. The act would change her into something else. This was the secret information her sisters had withheld. She felt giddy and off balance. She wanted to hold that long and secret part of him in her hands, stroke it soft soft, press it between her breasts. Mostly, she wanted to put it in her mouth.

Days went by, a quiet standoff between them. Back and forth to Miss Rain's house for more lessons, David going to fix the engine on his pirogue. More quiet meals around the table. He noticed she'd found a piece of string to tie her hair back with, and her face was more visible, more glowing and radiant. She liked to watch him smoke.

One day, he offered her the butt end of his cigarette and she took it. He made a sucking gesture with his mouth. She put the cigarette to her mouth and sucked, lightly at first. Nothing happened so she sucked hard and inhaled a large puff of smoke. She gasped and choked hard on it, coughed and spat and screwed up her eyes, and then she shook her head and glared at him.

"Sorry, sorry," he said. Her face went a strange greenish colour and he realised it was the chemicals mixed in with the tobacco that had disagreed with her. She went onto the porch and retched into the yard below. Harvey whined and barked at him. He nipped out the offending cigarette.

"Oh gorsh, sorry, sweetheart, I'm so sorry. Doh smoke again." She glared at him some more. Bad move. She lay on her stomach for the rest of the day with her head over the porch, vomiting up bile. He rubbed her back. Why was he so stupidy about her?

How does a humble fisherman seduce a mermaid? Do not offer her a cigarette and half kill her with its chemicals. Do not cook her fish. Do not covet her at all, in any way. Avert your eyes from her nakedness. Avert your eyes when she smiles, a smile that lights up every part of you. Do not expect to be liked, let alone loved. Give her your bed. Give her your clothes. Listen to her sing at night, songs of exquisite melody. Help her to walk again. Help her find language, any language at first. Hope her own words will soon flow. Don't be annoyed that your trusted pot hound likes her too bad. Don't fall hopelessly into a bitter-sweet tabanca because your feelings cannot be requited. She has lived for centuries in the sea. Who were her past lovers? Were there any? Who did she leave behind? Can she ever forgive the men who dragged her out of the sea, or the women who cursed her into it?

Rain came almost every day, and hard. They watched each other. She tried steamed vegetables, ate them quiet and dainty-like. He had understood that he couldn't set the pace. To give chase, or move too fast, would scare her off. He couldn't expect anything to be the same as he had known before with women. His days had burnt brighter since knowing her; he would have to wait this out, and even then he might not arrive where he'd been before. He knew no sweeter place than the hot and hidden sex of a woman. There was nothing more joyful than to put his head down there, between her legs, nothing of more delight than the sweet, sweet sexing in the blue hours of the night. Sexing had been his true calling in life. Not being a fisherman, or a damn singer with his old guitar; none of that. His true calling was to be a lover of women; he knew how to give them what they liked. It was a gift, a true calling, to be a pleasure-giver. He would cool himself and let the act happen in its own good time; when she was ready.

Miss Rain noticed that Reggie had changed since Aycayia's arrival. He'd never had such a friend before. Yes, there were other people, beside herself, in his life. Yes, he'd come across other children, but the sad truth was that he'd only been able to communicate, fluently, easily, with Geraldine Pike and herself. Now, after Aycayia's afternoon sessions, she and Reggie would spend time in the garden together, talking with their hands. Reggie had shown her the words of "Get Up Stand Up" by Bob Marley, and they would sing this together. In truth, she was picking up sign language a lot easier than spoken language, though her voice was like no other she'd heard. Aycayia spoke as if she had honey in her mouth. Pretty voice, in truth. Now and then she would sing a melody and Miss Rain would close her book, sit back and the lesson would cease, temporarily, until she had finished her song. The songs came whenever they chose to arise. Aycayia couldn't stop them; it was if they were cued up inside her, waiting in a long line, and every now and then one would emerge.

Miss Rain and Reggie had been a small, closed community of two before Aycayia arrived. No one came up to their great house on the hill, made mostly of cyp tree and mahogany—which was being eaten from the inside out by termites. The old stone steps had lost most of their mortar. The balcony in front was rotten and clotted with mould. The roof had lost tiles in the last hurricane and birds nested in the timbers. Now, they were a community of three. Every night Reggie went to bed excited and fulfilled. A friend. An ex-mermaid, a young woman coming to come and learning to talk his own language. So few, if any, could have bonded like this with Reggie, her talented, handsome son, whom she had cursed.

One afternoon, the wind picked up and the rain came into the house sideways. When this happened the porch flooded and Miss Rain and Reggie would hide inside and shiver and gaze with awe at the wildness of it all. The June rains, especially here at the tip of Black Conch, which poked out into the vast Atlantic and sometimes stood in the path of hurricanes, brought life for the next year, kept the island resplendent for the next season of dry. The earth drank its fill in four short months, and then it bulged, belly full. Sometimes, though, parts of the mountains and uprooted trees would slide down the sides of sheer cliffs and barricade one half of the island from the other. Black Conch people always kept a shovel in their car in rainy season. Rasta men and squatters living in shacks in the hills would often have to rebuild.

For Miss Rain, the roar of the rain was deafening and it made her reflect on how her son had no awareness of the sounds of danger. He'd never heard thunder, or a gunshot or a car backfire—or cries for help. Once she had tripped, fallen down the stairs, twisting her ankle, and he hadn't heard her hollering. Eventually, Geoffrey, the gardener, had found her. Miss Rain was always conscious that she needed to keep an eye on her son in the wet season and yet that afternoon, ambushed by the rain coming in sideways, when the blinds were flying about, a large pot of bougainvillea had smashed, and the peacocks had flown in to shelter, barking their insults, she hadn't noticed that Reggie and his new friend had disappeared towards the outskirts of the garden. There was a small white gate which led to a path and the path led towards the rain forest full of howlers and snakes. Miss Rain had been too busy mopping up the flood to notice her son and her student had wandered off the premises.

The pair had walked off, talking, long before the heaviest downpour came. The track into the forest was grassy at first, a clear path cut into it, and then it became steeper and less distinct. Then the rain started in and they ran for cover into the forest. Aycayia did her best in her size-nine Adidas sneakers. She followed Reggie, who ran towards the shelter of the old giant fig tree, Papa Bois, or so his mother said was its name. Though the rain bucketed down, the forest trees caught a lot of it, especially the leaves of the bois canot, which were large as plates. Even so, they were soaked. When they found Papa Bois, the giant fig, Aycayia stopped dead in her tracks and gasped. The tree was three hundred years old, Reggie told her. She nodded a 'hello' to the giant king, and the tree nodded back.

They huddled in the tree's gargantuan roots, roots which rose up from the ground like a labyrinth. Aycayia remembered the forests of her other life when she stood in the realm of trees and greeted them all. She had a feeling that the rain storm was because of her, that the rain was moving in off the sea, snarling up, wanting to snatch her back. They stood, drawn into themselves, gazing up at the liana vines hanging from the tree and the ropes of water unfurling from the heavens.

In the midst of this, Reggie was unable to quell his curiosity and wonder; he signed a question:

Where did you live before the sea?

An island.

Like this one?

Yes.

With trees this big?

Yes. Many trees this big.

This tree has a name, Papa Bois.

We had a name for trees. Then the word came, suddenly. Yabisi.

He nodded. Papa Bois is a story, he said. About an old man.

I am a story too.

Reggie nodded. Everything in the world had a story. He had a story too. He would write his story one day, and write about the mermaid.

Are you okay? he signed.

No.

Aycayia hadn't been able to express this sentiment before.

Reggie had guessed she wasn't happy. It wasn't a simple case of not being at home, or not being safe. He was seized by the urge to put his arms around her and he did so and squeezed her tight.

Aycayia hadn't been hugged in millennia. Tears rolled down her face. Then sharp peals of thunder erupted, deep rolling sounds, like the gods were throwing each other around. She realised Reggie couldn't hear this.

It must be scary being here again, on land.

Yes.

You are my first friend.

Aycayia nodded and a flow of unexpected feelings rose up in her, clamping up her throat.

I am happy to be your good friend.

Was it lonely in the sea?

They both stopped at the word lonely. Reggie had to make numerous signs for her to understand the word, until she nodded and her face clouded over.

There was another woman with me, Aycayia signed. She was old. She became a turtle.

I bet she misses you now.

Aycayia nodded.

How did you survive?

The lonely feeling?

Yes.

It was hard. It still is hard. I still feel the lonely in my body and my heart.

Reggie nodded. He understood.

When I'm twelve, I'm going to a school for other deaf kids. In America.

Aycayia clapped and signed that he was lucky; there were others like him. He would find them.

You find any other mermaids in the sea?

She shook her head.

I'm sorry.

Aycayia shivered. The lonely feeling was a terrible thing to bear. But the sea had been another kingdom; there were things she'd seen, wonders, the creatures she'd befriended there, the dangers that lurked, the orcas and the sharks. The sea was a silent but sentient world. She had grown to love parts of it.

It was then that a live carite hit the ground.

Astonished, they watched as it flipped and writhed on the muddy bank of earth. It had fallen from the sky, but must have come from the sea.

Aycayia let out a shriek, gazing upwards.

Another carite landed, *wap*. This too flipped and bounced in a frenzy of shock. They stared at it in horror, backing up against the wall of tree roots.

Another fish fell. Then another and another, until six or seven smallish silver fish had fallen through the sky, through the trees, and the ground was alive with thrashing carite.

They stared upwards. Was someone dropping them from the tree? Was there another person up there, in the branches? A person they hadn't seen? Was this person making himself or herself known?

More fish cascaded.

And then, an unmistakable cackle. The laughter of many

women up the heavens. Then the sky opened. Hundreds of silver carite rained down through the trees.

Reggie screamed.

The sky was dizzy with fish falling from the sky, a silver curtain in front of them. Like a fishing boat emptying its nets.

Aycayia grabbed Reggie by the hand and ran, dragging him away from the giant fig.

She sprinted on uncertain legs, as if the *diablesse* herself was chasing her down the mountain slopes and back towards the great house.

They arrived, chests heaving, shouting that fish were falling from the sky.

Miss Rain steupsed. She had only just managed to mop the porch and was vexed they were muddying it up again until she saw what a fright they had taken. Reggie made loud noises and his hands were forming many words at once, too quick for her to read them, something about fish. Aycayia was shouting, "FISH, they come for ME." She was dancing up and down and wailing. This upset the peacocks, who all began to hoot. Miss Rain put her hands over her ears at the clamour.

Then they saw it. A storm cloud had followed them. Small and high, thousands of fish were falling from it, like a waterfall of silver bodies, landing in her garden. Hundreds of fish were falling. The lawn, usually green and clipped, and bald here and there, tough old savannah grass, was flipping with the bodies of silver fish—carite, ballyhoo and God know what else.

"Holy Lord in heaven and hell," shouted Miss Rain, aghast. Then the shower ceased.

"What de hell . . . ," she muttered.

A single carite fell from the sky, zigzagging in a spiral downwards, like a ballet slipper.

Nothing more. Not a sardine, not a tuna.

Miss Rain's jaw dropped.

What was once a lawn was now a sea of fish, beating up. Then she heard it too. A soft cackle, high up in the winds.

Aycayia was crying.

Reggie was crying too, snot dripping from his nose, his mouth trembling.

"Bitches," Arcadia whispered. She turned to look at Aycayia, a woman whose story she could only guess. Had a curse been put on her, by other women? A curse that had followed her through the centuries? Jealousy, maybe, or something so.

She hugged Aycayia to her breast and shook her fist at the sky and whispered, "Oho. Okay. Okay, allyuh, right. We get it. We ready."

————

It take a long time to quiet myself after the fish rain
Power of the curse is no small thing
David came to carry me home
I went to sleep for many hours
I know then life on Black Conch island will be short
I am no longer what I was when I was a girl
No change one way and then change back
No hope of that
After the fish rain I realise curse strong strong
Women consult powerful Goddess Jagua
Curse stick to me even though they now long dead
Young woman self curse forever
No hope of happiness
I cry for some time
I know I have to return to the ocean

I take the conch shell on David's porch
to call out for my old companion Guanayoa
She will be waiting for me same same

I think of David a lot
I want to be a full woman
I am maiden still and I wonder
about those secret parts of a man

I dream of my death my dying
I think about killing myself
My own self death
I begin to think of that
I could hang myself
put an end to the curse
I begin to study that

I do not sleep since the fish rain
I dream the curse and the curse dreams me
It follow me to land and it follows me in my dreams
I begin to plan to end the curse
to kill myself on Black Conch island
That was where the curse would end

———

David Baptiste's journal, July 2015

Nothing came easy for her. But I notice how things shift after
Miss Rain tell me about the fish-rain cloud that follow her. I
never saw it myself, but I did see all of them fish on the lawn,

and it was hard to explain to the gardener, Geoffrey, a good fella from the village, a quiet soulful man. We ask him to say nothing. I carried Aycayia home and then went back to Miss Rain's house and between us we scooped the fish into four big garbage bags and we put them in the back of my truck. I drove them to the market in English Town to sell; no one asked too many questions and I got rid of them quick and made some money. Back home I found Aycayia sound asleep.

Later I hear she crying, like she fraid real bad. Like something still following she around. Till then, I figured she was safe, more or less. We would care for her, myself and Miss Rain, and in time she could go about in the village and, slow slow, everyone go accept her. Then—my plan—I would ask her to marry me. I even pictured our life together and imagined our children. Happy life—forever. I was wondering if I should say what was on my mind. But it look like she have real trouble on she back, like she bring it with her from her before life. And that old conch shell on my porch end up in her bed again. I still sleep downstairs, wanting to let her come into herself.

"I want to swimming." Those was her first words to me. She say them after the fish rain. "I want to swimming."

Them words surprising, believe me. You would figure she'd seen enough of the sea. But she hadn't.

"Take me to de sea," she said. Two months with me and she was learning our words. So, next day, with Harvey, I drove her down to a part of the sea that was quiet, and a time of day that quiet too. Sun rise. No one around. We walked down to the sea edge and she start to cry at the sight. My gut felt mix up. Me, a fisherman, and she my lady friend; the sea was our matchmaker. Till then, she only watch it from my porch, from far away. She kept her distance. Next thing, she have legs, but then is like she have no special equipment to help her swim. Just the body of a woman, like any other.

Lucky, no one was around. She peeled off what she wearing, and her sneakers, and ran down to the sea, with Harvey barking at her heels. Them was pardners, she and he. I understood they were making some kind of secret language between them.

At first, I watched. Although I can float and paddle about, I ent no swimmer, then and now. Fancy that, a fisherman who can't swim too good. But that's normal in these parts. So I watched as she and Harvey splashed about in the shallow part, near the edge. I felt happy for her. I didn't want to go in, not at first. But next thing I know, I drop my pants and stride in, in my drawers. I was in the water, up to my chest, and she, my mermaid, Aycayia, was floating naked on she back. She was smiling up at the sun. Her long dreads floated around her like snakes. Her tattoos made shapes under the water. Only then I saw she had come together, whole, as I ent seen before, like when she was a mermaid, half and half, poking the top half from the waves. Now, she was a full woman and she took away my breath. I had a cockstand good and proud under the water—though she didn't see it. I was glad for she and worried as well, in case she decide to change back into a mermaid right there and then and swim away. Harvey paddled around her, snapping at the water. Just so, I felt content like never before. She felt like family, like some part of me that had been missing all my life. I found her and she'd found me. Next thing she was in my arms and floating like a woman who was trusting and giving of herself. She let me hold her and float her on the turquoise sea. "You are not alone," I told her.

The fish rain had a lasting impact on Reggie, too. He didn't want to kill himself—that wasn't his response to his exclusion—but it had him cowed. The mermaid was his first friend, and it seemed that she might have to leave. He needed answers from his mother. They sat at the kitchen table the next morning, facing one another.

Who is she, Mum?

I don't know.

And that was the truth.

The other truth was that Reggie had not heard the voices of the women, the distant cackle.

How did all those fish fall from the sky?

Arcadia paused. I don't know.

Where did she come from?

I'm not sure. Another island. Long ago.

How long?

Long.

Millions of years?

No.

Thousands?

Maybe.

How did she end up with a fish tail?

She was cursed. By other women, I think. I'm not sure.

Why?

Arcadia knew Aycayia had bewitched her son, too.

You tell me, she signed.

Reggie watched her and then he gazed into his cornflakes. Eventually he said, Why did my father go away?

Arcadia blushed and her spine went hot. He'd never asked this so outright before.

You know I don't know, for certain.

Was he cursed too?

No.

Did you curse him?

No.

Was it me?

No.

Is this house a cursed place?

No!

Feels so.

Why?

Nobody here but you and me. Nobody comes. Only the mermaid and then she get chased by fish . . . I was happy.

Arcadia knew what he was trying to say. Something had happened that connected her and his friend. Some fate had interfered with her, as his mother, and with her happiness. His father, Life, had left her, abandoned them. Then deafness had happened to Reggie. It seemed like it was all part of something, but it wasn't. Life had left for his own reasons and Reggie was deaf by accident, and the house was just old.

You will be happy again. You were happy before.

Reggie pouted, unswayed. He was usually so full of light, so generous in his soul. She thought God had seen to that. He had an active imagination which served him well, till now. The mermaid had been his first love and the fish rain his first blow.

Will she stay here long?

I don't know.

Tell me about your childhood.

I've told you! Many times.

Tell me again.

Arcadia sighed. I was born upstairs, in the same bed I sleep in now. You were born in that bed too.

A smile flickered.

I was sent to boarding school, in Barbados, at the age of eleven. The Ursuline convent.

Reggie was beginning to light up. He loved this story, the story of how his parents met.

I had already met your father by then. Yes. We met as children. There was always your father. I knew him from before your age now.

You always knew him?

Yes.

From my age?

Yes, and younger.

What was he like when he was ten?

He was mad. Madder than you, or just as mad.

Reggie beamed.

You have the same face. We were friends, white girl and black boy. We didn't have a care in the world.

How did you meet?

We met at school.

Here?

Yes, before the convent.

Tell me the story.

You know it.

Tell me again.

He cut off one of my pigtails, in class.

Reggie laughed. The story was true. Life had snipped off her plait from behind, when the teacher had left the room. She had slapped him and he had laughed and then she cried. She was eight. Later, at home, her mother cut off the other plait to make it even. She went to school the next day with short hair. Little blonde girl, hair cut like a boy. Little black boy with a face full of mischief. Local primary school in the next village. Only forty children, and she the only white kid. They fell into each other's lives then, aged eight and nine. Best friends. Later, when they were teenagers, they would spend hours in the forest, naked, talking, and he would run his hands through her hair and laugh about the plait he'd cut.

I am a child of love, signed Reggie.

Yup.

I think he will come back, you know.

Oh? Why?

He must be remembering that I am the age you were, when you met.

That had not occurred to her.

You never know.

Truth was, she'd been packed off to school soon after, aged eleven. But their parting only intensified their feelings for each other. Seven years in that convent: the white-hot pavements, the French skipping, the decrepit nuns—their bloomers showing when they bent over to water the garden—the blue blur of Bajan sea, twinkling from far beyond the schoolroom windows. It was all made easier by the fact that she would elope and marry Life. It wasn't a fancy idea. It was how things would be.

And yet Life had disappeared.

He never said goodbye, or that he was going.

Heart-mate.

I will see my father some time soon, Reggie predicted.
Arcadia nodded. Ten years he'd been gone. Ten.
Okay, then, time for class.
Pythagoras?
No.
What?
Art.

7

Barracuda

≋

ARCADIA RAIN SLEPT WITH A GUN under her pillow. Her brother August had given her a Barracuda as a gift, a year or two ago, a small, wooden-handled six-shot revolver, an ex-law-enforcement pistol, light in the hand, easy to load and shoot. As a young girl, this brother had given her target practice, with old Milo tins nailed to a garden fence-post. She had practised and, over time, had become a mean shot. She even had a licence, but never flashed the gun about; it was just sensible to have as a backup. She was a woman alone and it was better than having a man about the place. A gun was a gun was a gun; no messing. The pot hounds often barked at night, but it was usually a passing car on the road that wound up into the hills. There had never been one actual intruder, but she slept better for having the Barracuda under her pillow.

For days after the fish rain, Arcadia hadn't slept well. Fish rained from clouds in her dreams. She dreamt of guns swimming through the sea. She woke up feeling a sense of loneliness. It was a loneliness that connected to the dormitory of the Ursuline convent at night, which stank of bay rum and ancient nuns; to this old planter's house where her parents fought, many times; to when her brothers departed after the hurricane hit in '61 and demolished the land; and, most of all, to when Life vanished. It was a feeling she never discussed; it was on hard lock in order to survive in this helluva place. She dreamt, too, of Aycayia strung upside down on the jetty, as David had told her. She remembered the American men who'd caught her—the virgin son who'd become possessed with some sort of conscience, and the father who wanted to have the mermaid killed. Something about Aycayia's arrival had stirred up all her old disturbances.

Then, late, that night, well after midnight . . . noises.

A clatter downstairs.

Slow, unmistakable creaking of footsteps on wooden floorboards. The pot hounds were whining, uneasily, but not barking.

Arcadia sat upright and listened hard. Whoever had come in had stopped. She felt for the Barracuda and grabbed it snug in her right hand.

A thump.

She leapt from her bed and tiptoed down the hall in her nightdress. She peeked in on Reggie; he was asleep, with his backside pointing upwards, as usual.

More noises downstairs. Someone was moving about, walking softly. Her palm moved flat to her throat. Where? In the kitchen? The hand holding the gun throbbed. She would use it in self-defence only. A single shot to the thigh. She would disable the man, then call Ce-Ce and summon the local police from the next parish, though they didn't even have a car.

Quiet quiet, she trod, barefoot. More thuds, as though the person had tripped over something. Did she hear a curse? The gun was loaded: six bullets; she pulled back the trigger and the chamber revolved. A bullet clunked into place.

The staircase was narrow and curved round a wall. At the bottom, she flattened herself and waited.

She heard the fridge door open. She heard a chair move. Her heart surged up into her throat. She gathered her nerves. She had no choice. She would shoot.

In a moment, she was in the kitchen and shouting, "Do not move one frigging muscle!"

She pointed the pistol straight at the dark figure of a man sitting in a chair at the table. No shaking, nothing; she would shoot the man if he made one single movement. Even in the dark, she could shoot straight: one shot, in the shoulder, take him down.

The figure froze. Shadows merged in the moonlight, but a man it was, boldfaced. Eating from her fridge.

"You put your frigging hands up in the air!" she barked. She made her way across to where the telephone sat on a pile of phone books, though she knew Ce-Ce's number off by heart.

"Up," she commanded. "Hands in the air."

Slowly, the man put his hands higher. Like he real cool with it, too, not afraid. Arcadia felt along the wall for the light switch and flicked the kitchen lights on.

"Jesus, Lord," she stuttered.

David Baptiste's journal, August 2015

Finally, when she came to me, it was sweet. I knew it would be. She came while I was sleeping. I didn't know at first if she was real or if she was a dream.

I wake up from a deep deep sleep, feeling that someone watching me. I open my eyes and Aycayia was kneeling there, on the ground beside my bed. Like she was praying over me. It was the moment I'd been hoping for, the moment I'd been waiting for all my life. A man have to wait for his bride; he have to wait quiet quiet for her to pick him. He have to stand still and be patient, for the right woman, and then the right time. I watched her watching me, like we been doing for months, from that first time I see her lift her head from the waves.

I say, "Come nuh, dou dou, woman, come to me, my love." She surprised me. She stood up and she took off her clothes. Slow slow, one garment and then the next. Then she stood in front of me, and the shadowy light of the hurricane lamp danced around her and she let me look at her for some time. I felt tears well up in my eyes to see her standing there so naked. She came to me, and it was as if a next woman had stepped into her and she leave behind that innocent girl. One step she take towards me and I was overwhelmed; was like a hundred women walk forward with her, into my bed, into my arms. I was waiting for her and when she came, she was a force of nature. Be careful what you wish for. Whoever say that is right like hell. Many women straddle my waist, many sit over me, drop their hair over me, and every man knows this is to see a woman in her full power. Aycayia come like some strong, sleek dolphin. She moved all in fluid movements and spread sheself over me, and she peer deep, deep into my eyes, into the soul of me, and she kissed me real good, on the mouth, and I say to her, "Come."

The small bedroom upstairs became a space of wonder. There, the young Taino woman, Aycayia, who used to be a mermaid and, before that, a young virginal woman, discovered the secrets her sisters had never wanted to share. First secret: how men kiss. These kisses, from David, mouth on mouth, tongues entwined, gave way to waves of warmth which swept down and then up again, bringing shudders on the upsweep, opening the flowers inside her, her womb, her heart. These waves of warmth opened her eyes too, so much so that all she could do was gaze at her lover, David the fisherman with the old guitar, while her eyes leaked with silvery light.

Aycayia let herself be kissed and kissed him back, trying her best to copy, and to be herself, knowing this kissing was the start of things and that there was an art to it. They kissed each other well and good for hours, mouth on mouth, and then other parts too, mouth on hands, feet, belly-hole, stomach, collarbones. Shins got kissed and big toes, baby toes. David kissed her webbiness, the opal pink skin between her fingers, and this sent shudders of delight down into her womb and her nipples burst forward and then David kissed one nipple, a slow sacred suck. Aycayia almost fainted at this pleasure. She had not imagined this type of happiness. Her breasts weren't big or small, but they had never been touched, let alone caressed or kissed, and the pleasure was deep and she lay back and proffered them for his attentions. They were covered in deep, inky spirals of the universe. David lavished on them tender caresses and he noted with pleasure how her skin raised at his touch. He had waited for this.

The night after she first came to him, they moved up to David's bed. She prompted in him a tenderness he'd never known. He had loved her on sight and now he'd won her trust. He was entranced, and slow slow he explored the wonders of her body, the hills and slopes and the curves. Slow slow, he parted her legs, the legs where once there had been a fish's tail, sealed off, banished and cursed for eternity. Slowly, he bent his head and buried his tongue between the folds of her sex and did what he was good at. Hours of adoration, he gave her, pleasure she could barely comprehend, and her body convulsed again. This was the second secret; the kissing men could do, *down there*. It was another art, another secret her sisters hadn't wanted to share. She had to be 'married' for it, so she never knew about its pleasures. All those men she had sent away, all wanting to marry her. Were they like this man, David? Would they have given her something like this? If she had chosen one, could she have been happy and not cursed? Could she have been content, after all? She remembered how the women in her village had gone to consult Jagua—the most powerful goddess they knew—after her banishment from the village hadn't worked, after their men still kept seeking her out, wanting to watch her dance. Jagua had called forth a tempest and she and Guanayoa had been engulfed and swept away to sea. For all her time of exile, she hadn't understood why.

In that magical bed, knowing how her body responded to his tongue, she finally understood why she had been cast away. It was because of this powerful feeling. This was what she had provoked in other men, the men of other women. She had never understood the why and the how of her curse. But it was something to do with this. It wasn't like anything she'd known before.

Then, a third secret was revealed. His long thing was soft on the outside, the skin of it, and yet it became hard hard like a tower, when he'd made her sex all soft and wet. Slow slow, he began to press it into her and break through into a space inside her. Then, he began his in-out-in-out rhythm and . . . her hips moved with his movements, and she began to melt away. This time she was nearly unconscious when the feeling of melting was complete. She understood even better the reason for her expulsion. Her gasps were ghostly whispers. Her body rode the wake of his thrusts. Oh! she exclaimed, and then she began to speak fluidly in her old language, as if this great power between them had unlocked the secrets of her past.

To David, this language from another time sounded ancient and yet familiar. It was sweet and soft, just like the way she sang her songs.

When Aycayia climbed on top of David, her long ropes of hair draped about him, her face lit up and glowing, David knew he'd met his mate, his lifetime companion. In one thrust, he released himself into her and she received his shuddering body, the ache of him, knowing then how lonely he'd been, too. They fell asleep, legs entwined, his long thing now soft but still inside her. Heads on the same pillow, they dreamt the same dream, of a time before time, when the islands of the archipelago were a garden, a time when no man walked here and all was peaceful.

―――――

Things I think about now
long time later
how heart feeling is stronger than me
stronger than a human being
I was banished from humans
then given the chance
to understand the WHY of my curse
with this man from the village of Black Conch
when we make arms and legs and in out sexing in his bed
Sea was calling me
Guanayoa was out there waiting
but I wanted to stay
Heart feeling last forever

though I writing this long time after I meet David
We spend a lot of time together in his small house
I would hear the women though
sometimes laughing quiet quiet
Heart was a magic power too
Stronger than them
After all I still feel heart now

———

Later, in David's small kitchen—a cold box and two gas burn-
ers, a drawer full of knives and forks and implements—Aycayia
tried to make herself useful. Maybe she wouldn't hang herself
after all. Maybe she could stay here in Black Conch with David;
maybe she could blend in, given time. She was a woman of the
Caribbean, after all; she had just re-emerged in a different time,
on a different island. The sexing had made her old self speak
her first language; she could get back there, in that magic bed.
Sexing had blown away the aeons of time that had killed off her
memory.

She filled the small tub with water from the barrel outside
the door.

Jiguera.

Toa.

More words in her old language would come. Back and forth
she went from the door to the tub and one by one she took the
plates and pots David had left unwashed from the night before.
She took a bottle full of green liquid, squeezed the liquid into
the water and saw it make a froth.

In her old life, they washed clay pots in the river, and women cooked on small fires. The men caught fish and other animals with spears and traps. The whole village shared what was caught; they ate from the land and the sea. They picked or grew what they needed; there was no green liquid and no plates, no trucks, no tarmac roads, no houses made of concrete, no kerosene lamps, no plastic, no metal forks or knives, no reggae music, no hi-fi or earphones, no Adidas sneakers, no clothes—nothing like these she had been wearing. She had watched the way ships had changed over the centuries, but she hadn't seen green liquid turn into frothy foam. She washed the plates and David's heavy metal coal pots with a feeling of careful disquiet.

By accident she pricked herself with one of David's sharp knives, a small prick, but it drew blood. She stared at the crimson fluid that seeped from her finger tip. There had been blood, too, in the bed; it had trickled from her legs, a small flow. Her finger ran with the same red. She licked it and wondered about being a woman again. Some new feeling had come into her, and from nowhere, and she knew it must have a name of some kind.

But she also knew she was a cursed woman since Reggie had taken her into the forest, since Papa Bois, since the carite had showered from the clouds. She knew then that she wouldn't be on land for long. She had contemplated suicide, a hanging rope. Now, as she tasted the blood brimming from her finger, her own body leaking out, she knew there was another problem for her. It was a feeling that went with all that toe kissing and in-out-in-out sexing, and the feeling was soft and warm, but it was also heavy and sad. She felt happy, but also trapped and forsaken in David's small home. The plates and green liquid that turned to froth—this new version of her life contained magic and there was this new feeling in her chest, strong strong, a feeling which she wondered about. What was it? It hurt, and yet it was sweet.

David Baptiste's journal, September 2015

I was a young man then and already had plenty sexing in my time on earth. I never consider myself so nice to look at, but somehow women liked me. I figure it was time to make a choice, settle down with one woman, and I knew it was with she, Aycayia, after she become a full woman. She and I was made to be something to each other. I was sure of that. I watch her slow slow decide to pick me. I never felt so proud. Then it come to me strong to make a decision to be just that for her. I wanted to guard her with my life. She would need that. Bodyguard, lover man. Husband.

I guessed the truth about the women who curse her. Sometimes, at night, she wake up for no reason. "You hear that?" she would say. I didn't hear nothing. "Voices," she'd say. She could hear them laughing at her, still. I wanted to keep her safe but I wanted her too, maybe just like those men she talk about in her past life. I loved who she was and how she make me feel.

One morning, when she was lying on top of me, naked, her eyes pouring light into my soul, her face lit with the wonders of our sexing, and her hair twist-up with mussaenda flowers she pick from trees in my garden, she sang for me. It sounded sad. I lay there feeling happy and sorry and all mix up. Afterwards, I think how an eternal truth come with her song, of how things had been in that time before time, when the archipelago was a garden. When she stopped singing, I felt soft and open in my heart and I said to her, "Please, will you marry me?" I said it without thinking, with the purest of heart, but when I say those words, her face cloud over.

I didn't see nothing wrong with asking her, but looking back I realise it was my big mistake. I was asking her for too much. I was asking her to lose her freedom, to be bound again. In a panic,

I was trying to keep her from leaving me, from disappearing back to the sea. I was impatient, troubled by this woman who was so hard to understand. I wanted to keep her safe, or so I told myself, but maybe I fool myself too; maybe "keep" was the problem. I learn things hard and slow. Man, you need to *give* deep feelings of affection and care, not keep them.

And so, it came to pass, that there, sitting on one of Arcadia's kitchen chairs, was Life. A large package, wrapped in brown paper and string, was on the table in front of him. Same, same as she last saw him. Long-jawed, knowing smile, eyes shining. In fact, he didn't look too different to when he was thirty years old and when he came all the time into this house, even when her parents were still alive. He had let himself in, as he always had. Arcadia could have shot him there and then. Could have shot this man dead who'd left her so suddenly, who she'd been devoted to since childhood, and whom she needed as a lover, a friend and a father for her son.

"Hello, hunny," he said.

Life still had his hands in the air. His face was alert and he looked at her straight, no apology, like their intimacy was right there in his eyes. Remember me? Yes, then she saw it, as she looked hard into his face, a trace of beard, some grey in it.

Hunny? Was he mad? She should shoot him for that alone.

"Ay, don't move," she said. But heat had ignited in her chest; her eyes were wet, she could feel them.

Life nodded, but he began to lower his hands. Eventually, she put down the gun, still loaded, on the pile of telephone books.

She pulled up a chair and sat there in front of him in her nightie. To begin with, all she could do was watch him.

It wasn't fair.

All she wanted to do was cuss. A great flush of relief in her chest, and a great flow of tender, oh so tender happiness began to mix up inside her and trickle out from her eyes, and yet she was vexed. Tears fell down her cheeks, and he saw them but he didn't move to touch her, not then.

"What's that?" she said of the package on the table.

"It's for you."

She looked at him: why couldn't he have rung? She could have collected him from the port in English Town.

He pushed the square package across the table towards her. It was a cube, a box, hand-wrapped.

She began to untie the knots in the string until they loosened and fell apart. Her fingers gnawed at the sellotape. She was a child again, opening a gift she'd never received before, not for Christmas or even birthdays, because she had spent so many of both in Barbados, at the convent. She pulled at the brown paper. How she could cuss this man, give him hell for this. His eyes were gleaming as the paper fell away in ripped-up rasps. She looked at him and then at the naked cardboard box.

"This had better be good," she said.

In the box there was shredded-up old newspaper and then, when she reached in, something hard and cold. With both hands she brought out the gift. It was a bust of a human head; it was heavy and red, red like the ochre red of the clay that came down the hill when it rained. When she examined it closely she saw it was a small sculpture of herself, her shoulders, her head.

"It's bronze underneath," he said. "The clay was laid over."

Arcadia weighed the cold red image of herself in her hands; it was as heavy, same face as hers, but another tint. She put the statue on the table between them. Why couldn't he just say "sorry"? Why couldn't he just knock on the door? What if she had shot him? What does a woman do with a man like this, eh? She'd held herself quiet for years. And all this time he sculpting some clay model of her?

"I made it a few years ago. I felt it belonged here. I brought it back. I'd been meaning to." His expression was hard to read.

"Come," she said.

He closed his eyes and she saw him check himself.

"Come, nuh. Come here."

He went across to her and laid his head in her arms and pulled her close and they hug up hard and soft, and he felt relief because he was tired from his journey and had been lonely for a long time. It was the price he'd paid for his freedom, a loneliness he hadn't expected to feel. All those other women he'd tried to lose himself in and with—they'd all melted away, one after the other. Life had lived a long time, a decade, without the love he'd known for this woman. He'd never really trusted her, a white woman, in truth, not once they grew to adulthood; and he had never trusted himself, either. Things had changed when they grew up and she had inherited the house and all the land around. He had needed to get away from Black Conch, away from this white woman, and all that meant. He'd needed to make his mark, discover his possibilities out there in the world. On the bigger island there were art galleries, theatres, actors, writers, artists. He wanted to know these people. He wanted to be one of them, too. But he hadn't allowed for his feelings, which had nagged and persisted for all those years, like it or not. When he'd heard there was a child on the way he'd fled, one night, on the ferry. His one chance for a new life. A child meant he would be bound to Black Conch and to his place in it, no matter which way he calculated it; he'd be put down, relegated. She was high and white. He had only ever snuck into the house at night, avoiding her parents, her brothers; it had been time to get out. He'd never expected his love for her to run him down. He laid his head on her chest and listened to her heart and he remembered who he'd been, and all their sexing in the forest, in this house. It was all mixed up with how he felt about this place too: Black Conch.

Aycayia puzzled over the question David had asked her. She didn't understand the new language she was learning well enough yet, so she wasn't sure, to start with, if she had understood him. Marry? What did it mean in these times? Did it mean the same as in her old life? She wished her six sisters were there to advise. Recently, she'd been going around the village cool so, mostly in the evenings, walking a little way up the long narrow road towards the next village; it was a lonely path of broken-up tarmac and she rarely met others on it. This question had thrown her into a blind chaos. She needed distance from David to think.

She left his bed, put on some of his clothes, a pair of his dark sunglasses to hide her eyes from the sun, and pulled on the Adidas sneakers. She picked up a bread roll and a mango. It was early in the morning; most people were still asleep. The sky was pale and it hovered close to the sea. The sea was dark and cold-looking, with small white caps on the waves. She walked out of the village along the road that hugged the seashore, climbing up, along the cliffs. She wanted to understand her feelings. She had never expected any of this: clothes, new legs, being able to talk in Black Conch parlance, making hand signs with Reggie—and a man to be with. She had almost come back to some kind of life.

She missed the sea, though. She missed the hiding she could do in it. She missed her tail. She had been a tremendous mermaid. But there was something in her old power that hadn't come with her, that had fallen off with her tail. On land she was a small woman. In the sea, she had swum alongside whales. As a woman she knew she was a little strange looking, what with her hands and feet; but she was getting by, getting to "pass" again as a woman. She had Reggie and Miss Rain as friends. She had been a graceful fish and now she was an awkward woman. Some of her woman was still fish, though: her small teeth, her salt smell. She couldn't stomach meat. She couldn't eat fish, either; it felt like eating fellow creatures. In the sea, she had fed on seaweed and plankton, conch, squid and small crabs. Even squid she rarely touched because they were so intelligent. Once, an octopus had been her close friend, a massive creature, a female, big as a carpet, muscly legs and a mouth that could crunch coral up into chunks. That octopus had lived a long time too, in the depths, under rocks. So all she ate on land was fruit and vegetables, some starch. It was enough. She wasn't the young Taino woman she had been before. She was the same age, a thousand or more years later, but there was the sea inside her; that was the main difference.

At a curve in the road, at the hip of the mountainside, she stopped to watch the sea. The pull of it flared in every cell of her body. It was a deep, satisfying, mesmerising feeling. She had seen hundreds of single-handed sailors, passing around the earth's watery surface, mad men mostly, not knowing where they were going or what they were doing. The sea was deeper than she knew or could swim. Her lungs hadn't the capacity to go to the ocean floor. Her time had been spent mostly in the upper sea, in its shallows, in its warmths. She considered her ex-life, her banishment, a life she had been put in and then taken from. Two things were true. She had outgrown it. But she was still part of it.

The sea was her home, and her exile. She felt passion for it and another feeling, too, close to revulsion. She was now part of the entire archipelago, land and sea. If she were to jump back in, she would be overwhelmed, she would drown, though she remembered the fight in her when caught with the hook.

And now this new powerful feeling in her life, a feeling for a man called David and this big question of "marry," which puzzled her.

Aycayia sat down on a bench by the lookout on the curve of the road and nibbled on the mango skin. She tugged it down in one neat strip, pulling it off. She ate the mango whole, down to the fuzzy naked stone. She munched the bread roll. David had made it himself, in what he called the "oven." He had learnt how to make bread from his mother, he once told her. It was similar to the flat cassava bread she knew and had eaten in her other life. Same, same. Cassava. Fruit. Things not so different in many ways. Earth still here; people still make bread. Sea still there; men catch fish.

If she said yes to marry, she could cook in a new way, in an oven. She had already learnt again what heat could do. She knew what fire could do to a potato, a yam, a pumpkin, or even bodi. She could wash the dishes with frothy green liquid. She could make passionate in-out sexing upstairs in the bed. But in her last life, men could have more than one wife; that was normal. Her own father had five; she was one of his many children. Would she have to share David one day? Maybe she and David could be happy together, but only alone for a short time. What would happen when he proposed marry to other women? She never wanted to marry before, so why now? If she didn't marry David, would she be punished again? Men only wanted to take hold of her freedom and keep it for themselves. No, she would not marry David; she didn't like the sound of it.

So she sang a quiet song to herself, sitting there, watching the sea rise and fall. In-out, in-out. She loved the sea, her safety and her prison. The sea rose, in-out, like sexing. Up-down, push-pull. All she could feel was this push-pull inside her. Yes. No. Yes to the powerful new feeling and no to the marry part of it. Was everything push-pull back on land? When they took her from the sea, those men in *Dauntless* had pulled her from her loneliness and also from her security.

David Baptiste's journal, September 2015

From when she disappear that morning after I proposed marriage, nothing went right. It was the only time I ever ask anyone to be my wife. I never ask it before or since. Looking back, I was too ahead of myself. She set off with a mango, a bread roll and a pair of my sunglasses, saying she was going to think about it all. I figure I shoot my mouth off big-time. I like that woman too bad. I like the funny way she walk; in some way she have grace, and in another way she was awkward. I like how she was at home with nature, the way she seem to know things I don't know, like she more connected to the earth. She liked to lay in my hammock on the porch, and I knew she had swung in a hammock before.

I lay in bed for a while, cursing my big mouth and feeling urgent in my heart because I was afraid about scaring her off. And I had done it, scared her good. I spent the morning mending a net on my porch, all the while thinking that maybe no fish ever need to get catch by me again. Maybe it was time to rethink how to get a living if I wanted to marry a woman who used to be a mermaid.

I was thinking these thoughts when Short Leg appeared, cool so, in front of me. He walk round the house and into my backyard. He was a young man, no more than eighteen, skinny and with one twist-up foot. I give him a nod and say good morning. He was usually a shy, don't-say-much boy. That day he looked like he have something to say. I know he was on *Dauntless* when they catch her. I know before he open his mouth he want to talk bout her.

"Talk, nuh," I say. I had a large needle in my hand and piles of net on my knees and the floor around me. I tried to sound casual.

He say he know who she is and I felt a sudden lump in my chest. I gave him a look which say keep talking.

He say he see she walking about now and then, how just this morning she walk past their house, how he recognise her from when . . .

I nod but keep my eyes fixed to the net.

He say how his mother tell him I have some cokey-eye woman living with me. I wasn't afraid of Priscilla, but she could cause real trouble if she want to. I ask him what he tell she back, and he just shift around on his lame foot. He claim he said nothing, so far, but then he come right out an ask, "Is true, then? Is she the mermaid we catch?"

I want to make him go away, for good, but he have more to say. He told me how he recognise her face, same face. Pretty. Indian, like. Not Hindu, red Indian. He ask me if she could talk now?

I tell him I have a lady friend staying with me, that she ent no damn mermaid, how she come from Jamaica and we knew each other long time and she staying by me. But Short Leg knew I was lying. The two of we let the subject quiet a little. I guessed there was a demand for a bribe coming. Then to make a bad morning worse, just so Priscilla appeared, with her other son, Nicholas.

I steupsed.

A gang, the three of them. Nicholas, of course, had seen the mermaid too. Priscilla already had a blazing look of triumph in her eyes. I remember well she was wearing pink rollers in her hair, had on a matching pink bra under her vest. She have that bad, bad look about her.

"Nicholas," she shouted, and she cuff him on the back so he flinched. "Say what you just say this morning. Go on, say it."

Nicholas look upset. He was older than Short Leg, maybe twenty, but only just. He look at me and then at his brother. They both look sorry.

"Tell him what you told me," Priscilla bawled. But neither of them boys wanted to talk.

"Oh, for Christ sakes," she exclaimed, and pull away my net and fix me with those bad eyes.

She say that the woman staying with me all this time, she is the mermaid from when those Yankee man come.

"That's who she is. That's what they tell me this morning. She a damn *fish*. And she been by you all this time. And she stink. I always know she ent just look fonny, but she smell fonny too. Like fish. She is the mermaid they loss. You tief her. Them American men, they go pay a big price for her when I tell them we found her."

In the kitchen, Life and Arcadia talked long through the night and into the morning. When Reggie came down for his breakfast, he found his mother still in her nightgown, which was unusual, a gun by the phone books and a strange man sitting at the table. He had short dreads and a beard with a little grey frizz in it, a little like the great Bob. Reggie blinked at the man and went to his mother's warm hip, and wrapped his arms around her. He knew in an instant this was him. The boy and the man locked eyes and gazed at each other. Neither of them was going to allow himself to cry, nothing like that.

Life stood up and said, "Hello, my son."

Reggie lip-read and nodded. But he wasn't going to act excited about this "son" thing. Unlike his mother, he'd been sure that this moment in his history would come, and had even rehearsed it.

It wasn't about forgiveness. It was something else. A decade of his life had passed, fatherless, when he actually had a father on earth. He wanted the man called Life, whom he'd heard a lot about, and who he knew was important to his mother, but he wanted him to figure it all out for himself. He wanted this man to know just how incredible he—Reggie Horatio Baptiste Rain— was, and just how okay he had been in his absence.

Reggie nodded at his father and smiled an okay.

His father had a lot of catching up to do if he planned to stay. And what if this surprise visit was just for one night? No, he wasn't going to let his dad know that his heart was galloping. Nothing like that. He stared at Life hard, drinking him in. Would he look the same when he got older? Did he have the same long chin? Life smiled at him and Reggie could hardly hold his gaze. He wanted to shout for happiness, but he held it all in— all the not knowing and the loss and the mystery of his father's whereabouts. His father was very good looking; like some kinda big shot had walked in. At least, Life wasn't a disappointment to look at.

Eventually, Arcadia said, "Well, I'm not going to sit here all day . . . What do you want for breakfast then?"

Pancakes, came the reply.

This meant a trip to the grocery, so Arcadia took away the gun and went upstairs to put on clothes, wash her face and comb her hair. She left her two men, men she loved beyond reason, to themselves and their man talk, two peas in a pod, same face, same lankiness, same shy-quiet thing, same charm. One deaf from her measles, her fault, a curse on him for his whole life, the other a damn vagabond. Both of them artists of one sort or another.

When she saw herself in the bathroom mirror, she gasped. She looked as if she'd had a shock. Her eyes were gleaming. She stabbed her cheeks with her index fingers, prodded her cheek-bones, bit one knuckle hard and screamed into it. He'd come back and her heart was swollen with love—her too damn easy heart. By now the vexed feeling had dissipated, though she knew it could swim back up from her belly.

They had talked all night, nothing more. That was why they had liked each other, then and still, having so many things to say to each other. That was why she'd missed him; he was her twinned universe, and she had missed the talking. You must not get happy, she told herself, while splashing her face. You mustn't get ahead of things; you mustn't get ideas. He had arrived, out of the blue. He said he'd missed her. So what? Men could miss anything. Reggie was beside himself, she could tell. Reggie would blow him away. Reggie was a miracle, too. Deaf or not. The mis-carriages before him. There'd even been talk from the doctor that she might never have a child. Slim hips and a womb prone to prolapse. Reggie had wanted to be born.

She slipped on a clean panty and a pair of denim jeans. She gazed out of the window at the sea, and she remembered Arnold on the jetty, with the marlin spike on his head and his premonition that the mermaid would bring trouble. That seemed like yesterday and it was months ago. In truth, the mermaid seemed only to have brought good things so far, though the dark significance of the fish rain nagged at the back of her mind. To think she hadn't believed those Yankee men. She'd been so lonely, getting by. She said a prayer for her son, and a prayer for Aycayia too, for she felt they both needed a prayer. For herself she whispered *Good luck*.

David Baptiste's journal, September 2015

Well, there was nothing I could do with the three of them standing there. Two of them could recognise her easy. All these years later, it seems absurd to write about it in these pages. It was absurd. I was hiding an ex-mermaid, doing just that, not only that, but I was in love with her. I went from boy to man in that year, but just how could she have blended in? Aycayia would never pass as human in every way. And those two boys who'd been aboard the Yankee men's boat know what they see. When the three of them came to confront me, I guessed they plan to say they going to inform the police.

I asked Priscilla, straight, what she wanted.

She said that my ass should be all in jail now. That I thief the people mermaid, take it away and steal it from them.

"I rescue her," I told her. She ent having none of the truth.

"You thief her," she say.

I try to appeal to her better nature. I say that the woman I rescue was a human being. But Priscilla ent have no better nature. She bawl out that the woman I love was a damn fish, a damn big mudderass half-fish, half whatever the hell she was.

A damn frikkin mermaid and she worth a million dollars and I thief her. Is me who want to make money. When I denied this, she called me a damn, boldfaced liar.

I try to explain, tell Priscilla her tail fall off quick quick . . . before I can put she back in the sea.

She give me a blazing look and say, "You even thief de goddamn tail," she said. "That thing worth plenty money. Where you hide it?"

I stared at her, disbelieving. People could be bad, yes. People could want to hurt other people's happiness. I stood up and put the net down. I was vexed. I said: "Priscilla, just what do you want to do, eh? What? You want to call them Yankee men back for she? You want to make some money? Eh? You figure she is that kind of thing? An object. To sell. To trade. Or is it something else?"

I know that Priscilla have more than one kinda reason for this challenge and she face set up.

I tell Priscilla to leave us alone. I even tell her the woman's name, Aycayia, how she come from another time and was cursed by other mean-spirit women, just like her. That was a waste of breath.

Priscilla's eyes glazed over.

"Aycay—who?"

But when I accused her of wanting to hurt me because she figure I cyan be happy with a woman unless is with her, I saw her eyes flicker. She stared me down hard. Maybe she shame to have the truth revealed in front of she two sons. She patted at her curlers. They give her a kinda pink halo, though she ent no kind of saint.

"The woman is a visitor to the island, from another Caribbean island," I said. "She same same, just like me and you, just unusual, looking a little different." I said that she wasn't no damn fish, not anymore, and I was going to marry her and if them feel to make trouble for me, then I go make trouble for them too.

The three of them gasped.

Priscilla took a step backwards. "What?" She looked astonished and disgusted at this idea. "You planning to marry a fish?"

We had never been comfortable neighbours, but I knew then I had trouble on my hands. Aycayia was still out on her walk on the road, and the worst thing that could happen was that she could bump into Priscilla on her way back to my home.

On the way back from the grocery, Arcadia spotted the figure of a woman walking alone on the verge of the road; she saw the long dreadlocks, the strange awkward lope. She was walking back towards the village. It was mid-morning and the sun was hard and loud in the sky. She stopped the jeep and shouted out to Aycayia, "Ayyyyy. Jump in."

They drove along in quiet comfort, though Arcadia could sense the younger woman had a lot on her mind. She wondered if Aycayia had had enough of living in Black Conch, whether she was homesick, not for the sea, but for the other island and other time.

"You out for a walk?"

Aycayia nodded.

"Do you miss . . . home?"

"Miss?"

"Are you remembering home?"

"I think of the sea."

"And before?"

"Yes. Home . . . was long time."

"I am happy you are here."

Aycayia gave her a careful look and took off her sunglasses.

"Ayyyyyy." Arcadia stopped the jeep; they were just outside St. Constance.

"Doh cry, sweetie. This will take time . . ."

Aycayia nodded and asked, "Are you . . . marry?"

Arcadia shook her head. "No."

"Why no?"

"Long story."

"David . . . wants me . . ."

Arcadia nodded, hardly surprised. It would give her some protection. "And you?"

Aycayia buried her head in her hands. There were things she felt and could not say. Miss Rain watched her for a few moments.

"Come up to my house," she said. "Come and have some pancakes."

"Pancakes?"

"I'll show you. Reggie will be pleased to see you . . . Come up, have some breakfast with us. I have a visitor too. My friend from long ago . . ."

Aycayia's face brightened. "Friend?"

"Yes, from long ago."

Life would like her. Arcadia knew that. In fact, Life would have the shock of his goddamn life.

Rain had started up, a mid-morning downpour, so the two women ran from the jeep to the great house, up the steps of the porch. Two of the peacocks were perched on the balustrade, huddled together, shivering. It could be cool up there, on the hill. Mist began to tumble down around them, closing the house in. Reggie had turned up the music and Aswad was pounding from the living room. When the women came in, they were greeted by the sight of a man and a small boy dancing, one with a pair of headphones clapped to his ears. Arcadia's heart caught in her throat. What with the rain and the reggae and the men dancing she couldn't say much; she stood there clutching the brown paper bag of pancake mix.

Aycayia was delighted to see Reggie. She joined the men, and the three of them grooved, Aycayia with David's sunglasses still hiding her mercury eyes. The pot hounds rushed to Arcadia's legs, wiggling their backsides, overcome with devotion. It was all because of Aycayia, Miss Rain was sure of that. She had brought with her a chain of events, and she felt both gratitude and compassion for her predicament. She would make no formal introduction between Aycayia and Life; they could figure each other out.

She took her groceries to the kitchen and began to prepare breakfast: batter mixture, coffee, some tomato choka. Life might stay more than one night. He might even stay a few. She must let him arrive. All those years, holding herself. Love could learn wisdom; love could guide her, and him too.

Arcadia heard a vehicle pull up on the drive. It was David, with a deeply troubled face.

"Come inside," she yelled, and he ran from the truck and stood in the kitchen, dripping.

He told her about Priscilla and her threats, that Aycayia had been identified by her sons, that it would only be a matter of time before everyone knew that she had been taken from the sea, that she was the mermaid the Yankee men had caught back in April, that she was worth lots of money and that it was he who stole her from the jetty.

"Well let people say what they want," said Arcadia. "Ce-Ce, all ah dem, they go be fine. Is just that Priscilla woman who go make a scene and I can take care of she. Long time she make trouble for people here. I can get her ass fired from Black Conch. She owes me rent, for a start. She figure she owe me nothing. But she can pack up and haul she ass outta here fast. Okay?"

David nodded but he still felt bad in his gut.

"Doh worry with that old, hard-faced woman. I badder than she when I ready."

David went inside and gasped. Jesus God on earth, where had his uncle Life come from? A tear of relief fell from his eyes. Life had come back! Life would make a difference. What was happening? What was happening in this goddamn village?

The rain pounded so hard it was difficult to hear each other speak during breakfast. The pot hounds huddled under the kitchen table. Arcadia had overcooked the choka into a dry-ish tomatoey paste, but no one noticed or complained. When Aycayia took off her sunglasses, Life's face changed from placid to an expression of wonderment. When she reached for the pancake syrup, he noticed her webbed hands. Reggie signed: She used to be a mermaid. She was caught by some Yankee men. In April. Uncle David rescued her. Arcadia interpreted. Life nodded but continued to watch Aycayia with an awe he couldn't hide. All in all, there was an air of occasion about that morning—all of them gathered there. Aycayia gazed at Life, with her calm, sweet innocence. He seemed to be important.

Two pancakes in, she said: "Who you?"

They all stared at him.

"I'm a man from Black Conch."

"You born in the village?"

"Yes."

"Home?"

"Yes."

She looked at Miss Rain, nodding. Reggie had the same face as Life. It was very noticeable.

"What is your name?"

"Life."

"Good name."

"Thanks."

"Better than Death."

"What is your name?" he asked.

"Sweet Voice."

"Nice."

Life looked at Arcadia, at how she'd grown deeper into her womanhood, then at his son, his poet son; no one had told him he was deaf, or how much he wore the same face. He watched the woman who used to be a mermaid, trying to take it all in. Things had really changed in Black Conch.

"You come love your son?" Aycayia asked.

"Yes."

"We are friends."

Life nodded and said, "Thank you."

"He teach me to talk with hands."

"I hope he will teach me too."

"Good." Aycayia smiled. "You will have to stay a few months."

Miss Rain gave Aycayia a look which said *enough*.

There was a buzz around the table. The rain made them huddle close, held them together. Reggie felt giddy with new feelings. Arcadia was overcome with a sudden rush of near but anxious happiness. The rain felt like a washing out of something. Late August. Soon, though, the big storms would arrive and this always made her nervous.

David, though, felt unsettled. With Priscilla and her sons on the warpath, how could Aycayia survive, let alone be his wife? What if she caught a virus? Could a common cold kill her? Could bush tea save her? He wanted to hold her hand under the table. When she looked his way it was hard to read her thoughts.

But it was good to see Life again. With Life here, Miss Rain now had a family. But would Life play into that? Would he become Reggie's real father? Men didn't do too much fathering around here. Could Life live up here in this big old house?

A peal of thunder cracked overhead and the pot hounds freaked under the table.

Aycayia looked up.

They all felt it.

Even Life looked up. "What the hell going on here?"

Aycayia fixed him with her big black eyes, silvery in the whites, and said: "Women curse me."

Life nodded.

"Not long I can stay here."

Life looked at David; he was different now, older, a man. He looked unhappy and he couldn't disguise how enraptured he was with the mermaid woman.

The rain started to come into the kitchen, sideways. It made them wet and made them shiver. The little dogs ran out from under the table, barking, running away from the rain. Arcadia rose to close the window.

Aycayia was looking around and it was clear she knew something they didn't. A strong gust of wind blew up through the kitchen. The window Miss Rain had tried to close banged open again.

Aycayia stood up and shouted to the ceiling, "Stop."

But the rain continued, and the wind howled through the great house. Aycayia jumped up on the kitchen table and raised her arms, shouting upwards, in her ancestors' language.

The roar stopped, abruptly.

The last of the rain fell in a long bolt. The sky seized up and dried. Aycayia continued to gaze upwards.

Everyone, except Reggie, heard the next sound. Quiet quiet and female.

Laughter.

The pot hounds barked at it.

Life stared upwards, and then gazed at the woman who used to be a mermaid. It was all finally sinking in: the very bad weather—it hadn't stopped raining since he'd arrived; this unusual woman with the webbed fingers who could make the rain cease with her unfathomable language; his son, who couldn't hear, but who'd arrested his heart in the very instant of their meeting; and the feeling that had sprung in his chest, his gut, his arms and legs, instantaneously, maybe even disastrously, for this white woman he'd known since her breasts were two pink jutting nubs, since her teeth had bands on them, since he had cut her pigtail off. He had always known her, known her from young, from even before the time of that big hurricane, from the years she came and went to Barbados, leaving him every time, twice a year, in those days of come and go—she the rich girl, he a poor boy. He'd known her from the time when they rushed at each other on her return, she bringing her stories of the Bajan sea, and they'd made love like daemons. Knew her from when they'd grown big and made a baby, their son, and he had left her, selfishly, when he needed to get away and be who he could be. All of that love, all of that time, mounted on him. It was more than he'd bargained for, especially now with the surprise of Aycayia, and Reggie, his son, so cool. Like it had all been organised, the way things had turned out. Push and pull. His heart caught up in his throat. What to say, eh? Maybe love had its own ways and timings. All he knew was that he was back.

8

Paradise

≈≈≈

PRISCILLA HAD A 'FRIEND' IN SMALL ROCK, the next village, in the police force. Well, he wasn't actually a friend, more a man who she had run down many times for sex and whose wife had threatened to kill her next time, but no mind that. Superintendent Porthos John was one of only three policemen in the northern tip of the island, one of seven on the whole island, and that meant a lot. Porthos spent his afternoons playing all fours behind the police station in Small Rock; everyone knew not to disturb the game. This gambling game was just one of the ways Porthos John supplemented his meagre wages. There was racketeering too; he had his hand in anything and everything that was going on, but never mind that.

When Priscilla arrived, she had taken the pink rollers out and brushed her hair, tweaking one curl down into a forelock. She had anointed herself with Jean Naté afterbath cologne and glossed her lips with Vaseline. It was late in the afternoon and the game was more or less done. Porthos hadn't won or lost, his stakes were even, and so was his mood. Her attraction to him was the only thing that was a problem. He was a giant of a man, once an army cadet on the larger island, and he spoke in a baritone which made her breasts jump. Between the voice and the uniform, she was done for. Long time they had been sexing, on and off. David was different. David was a younger man, unmarried, a local fisherman, nothing more. But Porthos? No. Porthos was she man. She hadn't seen him for a while, since all that thing with his wife. Porthos was one of the few men who could make her bad nature turn sweet, make her face blush with heat. He wasn't a regular Black Conch sweetman; he was a man's man, a man of the law, dishonest, as they all were, another woman's husband, and father of three. He was out of bounds, even by local standards, so for her he was sexy as a hunk of cheese with pepper jelly on a fresh Crix.

"Eh, eh," he said, when she appeared, all spruce and dressed up.

The other three men at the table smirked. One clicked his throat in anticipation of her tricks. Another sooted her through his teeth. They were local men who would take her round the back and give she a good brushing anytime, and they let her know it.

"Ay, guys, time to call it a day," Porthos said. Priscilla stared them down, like she'd come for business, like she would cuss each of them into a deep shame, divulge their innermost secrets if they didn't haul ass.

One by one they got up, each pretending they had something else to do, each feeling quietly usurped and curious in equal measure. Priscilla was like a wild mongoose in heat. The wife would hear of this, at the very least.

"Have a seat," Porthos said, pulling back one of the white plastic chairs. "Long time no see, what brings you here?"

She gazed at him hard through her lashes and he froze a little, knowing how she could get to him. She had stayed away, as she said she would, for two years now. Out of sight and out of mind. But not so far away. This woman, he feared, had some kind of shorthand way of connecting to him.

She drew up a chair. "I have something to share, something big. Das why I come."

He reached for his lighter and lit a cigarette, staring at her chest.

"Talk, nuh."

She told him about the fishing competition and the bacchanal about some lost mermaid two stupid white-ass Yankee men caught, that they say was thiefed from the jetty, and how these men then disappeared—one set of stupidness. Something she had no interest in. Until she met the woman with the cokey eyes living with the fisherman, David Baptiste, crawling around on the floor, like she cyan walk, and then she see her wandering round the village in her sunglasses and in Baptiste's tracksuit. Her way of walking around was all disconnected-like, like on tiptoe, like she scopsing something high up in the air. Like she not normal at all, not from these parts, and not even from Jamaica. And how her two sons had been on the Yankee men's boat and had seen this mermaid, in truth, and both of them had kept quiet about it, till the other day. Then they had seen the mermaid walking through the village, cool so.

Porthos coughed. "Allyuh been smoking something strong in Black Conch these days?"

"No."

He watched Priscilla. She could make up all kinds of stories; this was the maddest yet.

"Baptiste even want to marry this damn mermaid."

"What?"

"Yeah. He say he going an marry she, he even thief she tail. Maybe he sell it already. She worth millions. He thief her because he want she for he own profits. He say he marry her, but he thief she and he go own her and sell her someday. Just watch."

"Priscilla, you know this is mad talk."

"Long time mad things happen this end of the island. You know that."

"You say she's a mermaid, but is obvious she ent so any longer. Like she change back to woman. Fish part done."

"No. You can see her hands." She spread her fingers. "Like flippers."

Porthos raised his eyebrows.

"Her eyes real scary, boy. She look real old fashioned, like she been a mermaid a long time, or like she was an old-time warahoon woman from long past."

"What?"

"I telling you."

"So? Leave her alone; she not worth anything without she tail. She a woman now."

"Nooo. She's a fish. Or she used to be. I figure that bitch Miss Rain even teaching she how to talk."

"Well what you want me to do about it? She not breaking any law. She can be who she likes."

Priscilla flashed him an impatient look. "You really still ent getting it."

"Getting what?"

"Arrest her. Arrest Baptiste too, for possession or for theft."

"Eh?"

"He tief the people mermaid. That boat, *Dauntless*, must have been registered in English Town at the port authority. All American boats have to register in these waters. Name, address, phone number. Everything. Them men easy to reach, one phone call. Tell them we found their mermaid."

"Then what?"

"Keep her under lock and key, here in the jail in Small Rock. Tell them there will be a big fine before she release, half a million Yankee mudderass dollars. She has to be an illegal alien or something so, a damn illegal refugee. God, think of something! Baptiste is stupidy over her. I ent gonna live with her as my new 'neighbour,' pretend I don't know who she really is, am I?"

Porthos watched her and slowly he understood, yes, why she had come. Clever girl. Bad woman. Bad-minded, that was why she got to him, always. Cops and robbers. She was a badjohn, a robber woman, and that was the attraction.

Priscilla gazed at him and her blood stirred. Porthos was the father of her youngest son, Short Leg, born with one turned-in foot and his father's dark, searching eyes. She had never told Porthos because he never needed to know. He not playing father to her son; he have three children of his own, maybe more. He was her manfriend, her babyfather, her lover, nothing more. His wife was a dougla woman from the larger island, and she was a doormat, a housewife. It was she and Porthos who had been longtime lovers, on the side, long time before he had met his wife.

"I'll show you where she is. Okay? Lock her up. Ring them Yankee men in Florida. We'll split the release money half and half."

When David took Aycayia home and Reggie went upstairs, Arcadia went out onto the porch to look at the steep slopes of

Black Conch and its houses. At forty, the island was still all she knew; that and the Bajan convent. She had no reason to leave and nowhere to go. Ce-Ce and her family were like her own family, much more so than her brothers who never rang, whom she saw very rarely, usually only when they returned from the larger island, wanting money in the form of a piece of land to sell. Her home was this old house and her people were the people of Black Conch. One day her son would leave and join a deaf community elsewhere. That was a done deal. Reggie would get out into the world. But for her, Black Conch was yesterday, today and tomorrow. In a room full of books, in a house up in the hills, near a forest where she knew the howlers were harmless, she would live till her death.

Life joined her to watch the same hills, the bay. He put two fingers between her shoulder blades and stroked and she startled, and then softened. He sat down on one of the wooden-framed sofas which faced the sea and patted the cushion next to him. She gave him a look which said maybe, *if he was lucky*. He gave her his everything look, one he'd had in his face from a very young age, a look which said I'm a trickster, lover, wise man, good man, fool. She sat down next to him and eventually put her head on his shoulder. A breeze blew in, rustling the bamboo chimes. One of the pot hounds, half-spaniel, came and sat in front of them and stared. Its tail thumped softly. The sofa was big enough for Arcadia to spread out and she did so, laying her head in Life's lap. He stroked her blonde hair, curly, short—hair he had passed his hand through many times since the time he'd cut it off. He touched her ears, touched her nose, stroked her freckles. The dog groaned. Life pushed it away with one foot and it flumped to the floor.

Later, in the big brass bed, which had belonged to an aunt, in which she had been born and birthed their son, they lay down together. Life kissed the round curves of her belly, the sinkhole of her navel. He felt himself surrender to his want, his twin, his only real friend in the world. Home was her fingers, her elbows and her rib cage; home was her face, her eyes, her gaze, the way she said things, anything. He'd been so bored, so looking looking everywhere else but here. It didn't take long to find her current, her heat, an effortless tuning in.

"Come, come, nuh, come here," she whispered, and he kissed her soft on the lips, and then they came back to each other, tangled themselves up in each other's limbs, a lifetime of liking, of longing, with the sadness of years lost.

"I'm older now," Arcadia whispered, conscious of the silvery delta of stretch marks across her hips. Her feet had spread, her skin was no longer a satin covering. The sun had freckled her chest, her hands. A decade of loneliness had settled somewhere, but now this man was here again, with all his gifts.

It started to rain again, heavily. The room was dark but for the yellow glow of the night lamp beside the bed. Under the grey slopes of the mosquito net her thighs parted and his mouth fell on her. Her hand reached down to touch his head. Her hips rose and she looked up at the ceiling fan and tried to brace herself for more of him, and yet another loss, because a man like Life was too big for St. Constance. He'd never stay. She shifted herself to get close, to meet him. She remembered a time once, way back, the time she had first seen him, running down the hill, a skinny boy, looking back at her, grinning, mouthing the words, *Catch me*.

One morning, Aycayia woke up in a puddle of blood. The blood was dark and richly red, and it had blossomed from her womb. Her menses had started again.

"Look," she screeched at David, and showed him the blood on her fingers. She smelled it and then daubed it on her face. David laughed with surprise and delight. Her transformation was now complete. This was a cause for celebration. She laughed, too, and sang a joyful song and then pasted his chest with her blood. The blood had a metallic scent and he recognised it immediately; as a lover of women, he had known that scent all his life. He beamed at her.

"You come back a whole woman now," he said. She nodded and stood up, all bloody, and danced for him, crying too, tears of happiness and sadness and surprise, all mixed up. It meant she could have children, David knew. Would he now need to take precautions with her? What if she fell pregnant, she so young and fertile; what if they made a baby together and soon? He could barely keep himself from loving her in that way. Would they bring a child into the world? He wanted this more than anything. It would be his divine fate, a fisherman to have a child with this merwoman come from the waters around his home-land, the waters of Black Conch.

David Baptiste's journal, January 2016

I remember well the time Aycayia tell the rain to shut up, and it did. I hear the women laugh too, up there in the clouds, and it frighten me, frighten us all. I took her home and ponder hard on our situation. She'd been staying by me, what, all of four months. She could walk and she could talk in a broken-up way and yet she still wasn't quite normal. She was what she was. Her menses, they came back too around that time. I figure next thing was that she could end up bellyful; and then what? I could be a father too, and that thought made me feel happy and scared in equal measures. The subject of wife and marriage fell by the wayside. We make love for hours every night in that bed, the bed I still sleep in. She fit me in some hard-to-explain way, fit my body and my soul. I tell her I will keep her safe, care for her always, that we can even leave Black Conch, move to a next part of the island, or even another island, to get away from Priscilla and her bad-mindedness.

Next morning was the beginning of the end of things.

Aycayia wake me up, screaming.

She pull back the covers of the bed. It wasn't blood this time. Nothing to celebrate.

Like an allergy had broken out. Her legs were covered in scales, fine and glittery. My first thought was to pour some sea water onto them, to make the scales go away. I figured is like a rash, like she get upset and have a reaction to the clouds laughing, but Aycayia look at me with a terrible knowing in her face.

"They come for me," she said.

"No they can't, they dead," I replied. But she frighten the curse was still alive, that she was changing again. And she leap out of bed and pull on some clothes and then, before I could stop her, she was out the door and running fast fast towards the hills above Black Conch and the rain forest.

"No," I shout after her. I ran outside in my yard, wearing only my drawers, and look up the road, calling, "Don't go! Where you going?" I beg, but I only see her vanishing round the corner.

I assumed she would come back, like she had before. I shoulda run straight after her, but I let her go. I figure she wanted to be alone. I figure she was scared. I was too. I lit the stove for coffee and I meditated. Her legs were shimmering. That was fish scales I'd seen. What if she was turning back into a mermaid? What then? How would we cope? How would I cope? I tried to think of the worst-case scenario and this only made my legs weak. I sat down on my porch, looked out over the sea where I first seen her, where those Yankee men hook her, club her down, bring her back half dead.

But she didn't return that morning. By midday, I was worried. I took a cutlass and pull on my old boots and head towards the hills and the forest. I knew she'd gone up there once with Reggie, and they visit the big old tree they have up there. Papa Bois. I had a hunch she gone back there and so I head up into the rain forest, as old as the time before anyone arrive by canoe from the Orinoco.

Swim the sea all alone now
Reggie show me Papa Bois
I can speak to trees
I think the tree can save me
Ropes hang down from tree

A curse lasts forever
To make a curse is to make evil
Never curse another
Think of me if you find this letter
and read my story
Aycayia the mermaid from the island
shaped like a lizard

Paradise

I was cursed by jealousy to be alone
a mermaid with no heart feelings
I was banished before I could be real woman
Blood come back
then fish scales
Full change to woman
and then change back to fish
Guanayoa my companion
She is still with me today
That day I try to kill myself well and good

I will live until there is no more water in the sea
I am now and forever
I will be here for the whole of time
I, Aycayia Sweet Voice

Heart feeling was my knowing on land once
in the island of Black Conch
I was the mermaid who lived there once
I was the mermaid of Black Conch.

———

When Superintendent Porthos John and Priscilla arrived at David Baptiste's home at lunchtime, late August of 1976, there was no answer to their knocks. They walked around to the back yard, stood on the porch and peered in.

"Nobody home," said Porthos.

Priscilla steupsed.

"You know anywhere else they could be?"

"Yeah."

"Where?"

"Only one other place. Up by Miss Rain. She does be up there every afternoon. Das where they must be. Miss Rain's man come back to Black Conch, only the other day."

"Who?"

"That long-face man. Some artist. He left here long time. Horn she bad, left she white ass. They say her deaf son is his son."

Priscilla watched for his reaction but there wasn't one.

"Life? You mean Life, that wild man from round these parts?"

"Yeah. Him. Long-face man with big ideas. Long time he left."

"How you know he back?"

"Is Black Conch, nuh. He roll in the other day. Hard to miss a man like he coming through. He have a few drinks down at Ce-Ce, saying he only staying a few days. He bound to be up at Miss Rain's too, if I know him."

"I knew Life."

"Yeah? You and everybody else round here."

"You think they up there?"

"Worth a check."

"I ent ever been up to that house."

"Neither me. That bitch does keep herself up there high and mighty. Looking down on she subjects."

"I hear she not so bad."

Priscilla gave him a fierce face, passionate with hatred.

"Calm down, gyal," he said teasing.

"Calm?"

The heat from her was palpable. It was the thing he liked about her most, her passionate nature. She could be badder than a hangover on a hot day, more sour than a force-ripe pomme-cythere, badder than most bad men he'd met, and her hatred of white people was her baddest part of all.

"Come nuh," said Porthos. "Lehwe go pay Miss High and Mighty a visit." And he gave her a look which said *and later I'll pay you a visit too.*

Priscilla's face broke into a smile wider than her face. They hopped into the small brown Datsun Sunny, which was on un-official long-term loan to the station, the only police car on the island. It had a green Perspex strip across the top front of the windscreen on which was written the words Natty Dread.

When Aycayia reached the giant fig tree with the roots as high as walls she sat down beside it, and remembered. Her father, the great chief, her mother, his third wife, the village she had known all her short life, the great square house her family lived in, the zemis of their gods, the ball court, the great feasts, her sisters and her halfs, the other women in the village and their men. It was aeons ago and yet their faces emerged from her memory. Her people were not the first people of the archipelago. They came from them, born from a long line that had arrived by canoa from the centre of the Americas. They had adapted to island life, though there had been great killings even before the Spanish admiral arrived with his guns and lust for gold. These islands had been peopled and re-peopled more than once. Her people knew how to live mostly at peace with the great kingdoms of the world around them.

And yet, she'd been punished. She had been cursed for the problem of the heart-feeling, the in-out magic of bed, those feel-ings she now knew with David. Even long-ago people could be bad. They could be jealous. Women had sealed her off, thrown her into the sea, and cursed her with perpetual virginhood. Stay in the sea. Stay away from man. No heart feeling in her chest. She knew she would soon be back in the ocean, back to her loneliness. She could feel the beginnings of a reversal in the atoms of her flesh, her turning back to mermaid. The sea had never washed out of her. The pulling back had been present all these months on land. The curse had been all too effective. Those women had not fixed a time limit. Her exile was for eternity; that had been their intention. Go away forever, until the planet burnt to dust, like other planets had, or the ocean dried up. David had told her there were many stories of mermaids in the world, but for people now they were just stories. No one believed these stories came from real life. But every man and woman on earth had a short life. Seventy cycles, maybe more. So mankind, even together, had a short memory. Death came to find people in many ways, at any time; life on earth was always a short stay. On earth, man or a woman could utter a curse and they and the curse would die. But this curse had no end.

Glittery scales had sprung up on her thighs, overnight, since she'd heard those women laugh. fish self coming back. First the flow of blood, then the scales come back. Good joke. Those women were treacherous. Soon her legs would seal up again, woman skin would disappear. How long? Days? Weeks? How best to beat her fate? Thick liana vines fell from the giant fig. It wasn't hard to reach one. She tugged hard at a vine that dangled in the air. That would be the best way, but the vine fell below head height. She would find a higher one.

When Porthos and Priscilla drew up at the great house, Porthos said, "You stay here for now, okay?"

Priscilla steupsed and gave him a look that ravished him dead.

"Okay." She nodded, looking away.

The house trembled a little in the furnace of the midday heat. The porch spilled a magenta stream of bougainvillea onto the lawn. The walls of the house peeled and flaked with mildewed paint. The white peacock strutted the lawn and Superintendent Porthos John braced himself for the whiteness of this old piece of the island. Decayed as it was, it still showed it had been built to dominate. He had heard from Ce-Ce and her brothers, from others around, that Miss Rain was okay. They had passed each other many times on the road, she with her deaf son next to her in their jeep. Other men on the force had dealt with her, too, now and then. She had a licensed handgun on the premises, that much he knew, and there had never been any trouble up here; no one would dare break in given that she owned almost every damn person's home, land, livelihood for miles around. To hell with it that she was . . . benevolent. Damn bitch owned everything, high and white, just like her ancestors. Slave days done and yet the house up here on the hill, hidden, gave no welcome to people like him, though it had been built by black men, ex-slaves. It had been serviced by black people yet never had a damn black man sleeping under its roof, at least not one who stayed. Temperance was its name, but it had been a mistake to call it that, some old white man's delusion.

He tooted the horn and didn't wait to be let in. He opened the gate and the pot hounds swarmed around him like a bunch of happy sheep. He kicked them off and set his cap straight and struck out towards the white people house. On the porch he found the place quiet. Her jeep was parked up nearby, but it was as if nobody was home, or maybe everybody was asleep. He rapped loudly on the windowpane and peered in. The main room was bigger than his entire house, and full of books.

"Hello?"

He turned to see Miss Rain standing there, in a housedress and apron, barefoot.

She stared him down. First time policeman ever come to her home. Damn man let himself in. First that Yankee fool, then Life sneaking in, dead of night, and now the police.

Porthos glared at her. She was short, even small. No matter. "I'm here on some . . . delicate business."

"Oho." The man was big, a giant, but so what? Miss Rain looked towards his car, saw another person in it, but could not see who it was.

"Well, it better not be about no damn mermaid, okay?" She gave him the sternest cut-eye she could.

Porthos John felt a certain chill strike his bones; he felt this every time he knew someone was lying. He was a gambling man and he knew this woman was bluffing through her teeth.

"So. Miss Rain."

"Arcadia, for God sakes."

"A boat called *Dauntless* arrive here in Black Conch back in April, the twenty-second, to be precise. For the annual fishing competition. Boat owned by the name of American banker, Thomas Clayson."

"Never heard of it."

"No?"

"No."

"Two white men. They hire local men as crew. Men you know."

"So?"

Porthos John glared at her, sizing her up. She had spent her childhood away in Barbados, people said. Her parents had been drunks, both freckly-faced too, in the way Caribbean white people could get, dead long time from skin cancer which started in the face.

Arcadia knew a bribe wouldn't work. Everybody could bribe the police round here, but not her.

"These men caught something unusual. It caused a stir."

"Yeah, I heard."

"I have witnesses."

Arcadia watched him. Who was in the car?

"The two young men on board that boat say they've seen her."

"The famous mermaid of Black Conch? Really? Well then, good. But that was a long time ago, April time. Maybe they did catch a damn mermaid, but she went back, or someone cut her down. Maybe they ate her, or they let her go, God knows, and I, for one, don't care."

"My witnesses say they saw this mermaid woman alive. Yesterday. Alive and well and living in Black Conch."

A hard ball of air caught up in her throat. It was then she saw Priscilla coming across the lawn like a rocket. She flew up the steps to the policeman's side.

"David Baptiste hiding this mermaid he tief," she blurted. She blazed a look of righteous certitude in Miss Rain's direction.

"Baptiste been hiding her in Black Conch, all now. My sons saw her on them Yankee men boat and then, the other day, walking through the village. Plain view. Baptiste tief them Yankee men property. Now he disappear, and she too disappear. Where he take her? Eh?"

"Get off my land," Miss Rain said, cold cold.

Priscilla laughed and she mimicked a queen from a foreign country. "Your land, is it?"

Arcadia prickled. She gazed at them. This was why she kept

to herself, to keep away from this hatred. History. The great tragic past. Her family had not been owners of slaves, but they had benefited from the whole damn thing, like it or not; they were part of it, and the house, crumbling though it was, said it all.

"The earth itself? Eh? Trees? The focking parrots in the trees? The frogs in the trees. Dey belong to you? Eh?"

"Go away," Arcadia whispered.

"No."

"What?"

"Make me."

Porthos John straightened up and they both gazed hard at the small white woman who owned everything from centuries back.

"You go. You and your whole damn friggin family. Why don't you go back on de damn boat allyuh came on, back to Eng-uh-land. Get the entire fuck outta we country."

Miss Rain blushed hard and felt a hot shame.

"You ent get to tell us where to go and be and what not to do with a mermaid. She have a price on she head. You telling us not to look for she. You? With all this land and money and you feel is for you to keep us from making money too?"

"I know nothing about this mermaid," Miss Rain said, deciding she was going to get her gun.

Porthos stepped in. "Look, if such a mermaid was caught," he said, gazing around the grounds, "and if she is indeed still in these parts, then the very least I'm obliged to do is search for her. The Americans caught her fair and square. Whoever took her has committed theft. And whoever is hiding her is aiding and abetting property theft. I will issue a search warrant, if need be," he said, searching her face, "of your premises. And an arrest warrant for anyone found harbouring an illegal immigrant or stolen property."

"She's no longer a mermaid," said Miss Rain, quietly.

Porthos John stared.

"She's a woman again, just like she once was."

"Where is she?" said Priscilla.

"I don't know."

"You been hiding her?"

"No."

"You been teaching her words?"

"Yes."

"Here?"

Miss Rain nodded.

Priscilla gave Porthos the nod. "See? Arrest her."

But Porthos was mesmerised. "What?"

"Yes, those Yankee men pull an unfortunate creature from the sea. David Baptiste rescue her and want to put her back. Then she was stuck here. In Black Conch. With no family. Nothing. No way to get back to who she was. Yes, we hope to give her some space to grow back, become herself again, in any way she can. But that's not so easy. And she's not so safe here in Black Conch, after all. We hoped she could maybe even blend in. But not everyone so . . . charitable."

"How all this happen?" Porthos exclaimed. Up till then he was not entirely sold on the mermaid story.

"She was cursed. Centuries ago, by some women. Cursed for being young, for her beauty; that's what I worked out. I ent even believe it, till I saw her and met her. Her name is Aycayia. She comes from Cuba or somewhere up there, and she's been living here for a few months, but God knows for how much longer."

Porthos mopped his brow.

"The curse has followed her here."

Priscilla was having none of it. No feeling sorry for the mermaid or this white bitch hiding her. "Curse?" she said. "Curse?"

Miss Rain nodded.

"Let me tell you about curse." And she screwed her eyes tight. "I curse this house. This damn focking planter's house high up here atop de mountain on which it was built by black men for you white people. I curse the wood it was built with. I curse the rafters holding up de roof. I curse every piece of wood and every stone that make this house a safe place for you and your goddamn family to live and rule. I curse your home. I curse it well and good. Damn this house to hell and may it soon be destroyed and everything with it. Damn you, damn your family and damn your home, Miss High and White."

Miss Rain shuddered. "Get out," she said. Priscilla smirked and spat on the ground.

"Let's go," said Porthos, nodding; he was scared and unsure of how to proceed with these unfolding events; he was unsure of himself for the very first time in his life.

9

Operation Nauticus

≈

David Baptiste's journal, January 2016

I still see her naked body swinging from a vine from that giant tree in the forest. My heart went dead in my chest and I bawl out *No* and ran to her.

I cut the line with one swipe of my cutlass and her body fell to the ground. "Wake up, sweetness, wake up," I shout. She lay there naked in my arms, between life and death, eyes closed. I said my prayers to God for help. Her face looked quiet as the sea at dawn.

"Wake up, sweetness, wake up," I said again and again. The tree looked like it was crying too, weeping over us. A man come upon himself only now and then in his life, and that was one of those times. I shoulda run after her, I shoulda watch over her better.

"No, sweetness, dou dou, heaven. No." And I hug her close to me and then I felt her heart still beating.

She opened her eyes. She tell me, "No. Let me die. Let me beat the curse put on my head. I won't go back into the sea again. Let me die now."

Shit, man.

I was wretched for her, and for us. Those women had followed her with their damn curse.

I could see more of her skin turning back to scales, shimmering there, under the tree. "No," she kept saying. I wondered if I'd made the wrong decision. One or two minutes later and she would have been dead. And free? I will never know that.

I sat for a long time under the big tree with Aycayia, Sweet Voice, sweet love in my arms, sitting quiet quiet, wishing the forest would take us in its arms, too. I wished the tree could save us. I sang to her the same old tunes I sang when we first meet. Man could hate other man, *oui*. Woman could hate other woman. But the soft feeling I had inside me was like a force, and it has kept strong all these years since that terrible day in the forest. I wonder about a time when no one lived in these islands, when trees and nature keep to itself. I sang to my sweet, sweet love. I sang her songs of harmony with the earth, and waited for her breath to come back and for her body to warm up.

Next day, well before dawn, when everyone was still sleeping, Superintendent Porthos John arrived at David's house with six men, heavily armed with four machine guns and two arrest warrants. They were dressed in full S.W.A.T. fatigues. This was Operation Nauticus, its aim to capture the dangerous malevolent half-whale creature that had been secreted away all this time in Black Conch, without his knowledge, without a visa, with nothing to show for herself, a threat to the community with her diseases and whatever came with her from the sea. He would return her, once heavy fines were paid, to the foreign banker who had captured her and then she would be off the island, no longer his responsibility. He would eliminate her from the vicinity. It wasn't like he was selling one of his own people; she wasn't from Black Conch. No. She wasn't even human. The fisherman would face charges of theft and harbouring an illegal alien. Miss Rain would face charges of aiding and abetting and perjury. Superintendent Porthos John would have all of them in court, for sure, and soon.

One thing at a time, though.

First thing was getting that damn slippery fish back to the jail in Small Rock. Five am. Dead-of-night operation. He had to call in three of the other policemen on the island. They had borrowed the S.W.A.T. outfits from an old army cocaine-sting operation years back. The guns were ancient and two were empty of ammunition. The trucks were retired army vehicles, tyres bun.

David and Aycayia were lying in each other's arms when a hard rapping came at the door. Voices at the porch, then a smash and the sound of men coming in through both doors. It all happened fast. Men thundering upstairs, four of them surrounding the bed, flashlights shining in their victims' faces. The men were wearing balaclavas. One man pulled back the covers of the bed. David and Aycayia were naked. They gaped at the sight of the scales shimmering up Aycayia's legs and torso; three of them backed away. Jumbie woman, or something so.

All three pointed their machine guns at Aycayia.

"Hands in the air," one managed to shout.

Porthos John came up the stairs and gazed at the sight of the naked mermaid. His stomach turned.

"You are both under arrest," he commanded.

Then he crossed himself. Not in all his years of policing had he seen anything like this. This wasn't one of Priscilla's tricks, after all. It was a goddamn freak of nature. He had read about such things in *Ripley's Believe It or Not!* Now he had seen this aberration with his own eyes.

David and Aycayia got out of the bed and the policemen stared while they dressed themselves. Porthos looked away.

"Get them into the truck," he said.

David knew Porthos and gave him a dead look, eye-to-eye, man-to-man, a look that accused him of betrayal.

Aycayia began to weep.

All the men felt guilty.

"Shut up," Porthos said.

Operation Nauticus had been successful so far. In one of the trucks the suspects were handcuffed, their hands bound behind their backs. It was still dark; no one had heard them. The two trucks rolled quietly out of Black Conch. Porthos John sat in the cab of the truck that carried the prisoners, his heart beating up like a carite in a net. He put his hand to his chest to try to stop it. He hadn't expected to feel what he was feeling now. Like it was *he* who was caught. But he said nothing as the trucks made their way on the narrow broken-up road to Small Rock. There would be phone calls to make and paperwork to do. The jumbie fish woman wasn't what he had expected; she was so small and so . . . young. Same age as his eldest daughter, same shy face. As Miss Rain had testified, she was a woman now, a young gyal. But it was clear something was happening to her. She was changing back, something so. He would call these Yankee men straight away, get them to Black Conch as soon as possible. No one had seen his men come and go at dead of night, no one would know they were holding the woman and Baptiste in the basement cells at the back of the station house. He would get her off the island, off his hands within forty-eight hours. He would make a good piece of money out of this, and then maybe he could quit his job. Move south to English Town, buy himself a business, open a shop. All these years he'd been playing cop when there was almost nothing, no crime to keep his eye on in Black Conch. Those games of all fours, his tiny wage, the extra money he pulled in here and there on the side—it was a pittance. He was forty-five, a good time to retire. All he had to do was just hold himself together till them Yankee men arrive and take her off his hands, pay him a big fat cheque to keep quiet.

———

I try to end my life to end the curse
David stopped my death on earth
Papa Bois did not save me in the end

Then we get caught
Police want to sell me back to Yankee men
from *Dauntless* canoa
Me and David locked up
Fish self coming back
The story in a nutshell
My short time in Black Conch soon over
David and me sit in the cells watching each other
That was a black night
I still remember you, David
I still swim past your house
I still come to Black Conch
No more guitar loverman
No more secrets of in and out
No more Miss Rain Reggie and Life

The voices in the clouds were laughing
all the time we were in the prison cells
Curse is for ever
the mermaid of Black Conch is a cursed creature

———

Porthos John stood watching the captives for several moments as dawn began to break: one small woman turning back to a mermaid and this man, David Baptiste, a local fisherman. Deep down, in his balls, he knew he'd done something unjust. This young woman was some kind of half and half; he should leave her alone, let her be. Then he reminded himself about the money. A new life. Maybe he could divorce his wife. Leave her in Small Rock, start again with some nice young thing.

Priscilla was upstairs in his office; she was happy. Miami was an hour ahead. They would wait an hour to call. Porthos went upstairs and watched her. They had pulled off something big. Cop and robber woman, they were a pair to be reckoned with. Then they heard it: a sound like laughter, high up in the clouds. It electrified his nerves, made his skin rise up in terror. He wanted the Yankee men to get her off the island now.

"Whoever she is, she trouble no ass," he said in a grave voice. "I want that woman, fish, whatever she is, gone, okay? Gone, as soon as possible, before she bring bad luck on my head."

Priscilla sat in his office chair, one leg up on his desk. One hand rested on her pussy. She gave him a look from way back, from all those times, a look he couldn't resist.

"Come," she said.

In a moment they were bent over the desk, joined, his S.W.A.T. trousers on the floor, cuffing his legs together at the ankle.

She was warm and deep and her kisses stole away his will-power. She didn't love him and that was a badness in itself, irre-sistible, to be so warm and deep and unloving.

"You badness self," he whispered.

Life lay in Arcadia's bed with his head on her stomach. They were weak from loving each other, after all this time. She had finally surrendered and let go. Her womb was soft and her heart was open and her head was on fire with it all. It wasn't possible to hold on to any kind of 'no' in the face of Life's tender power. Words of love flowed easily between them, till they came upon the truth of it all: a lifetime of loving and knowing each other up there in the hills, in this house and all around. They were mature adults now, with a child to prove their feelings. Until then, the nature of his return was a subject not to be mentioned. How? Where? A plan would be needed and Black Conch men did not commit to plans. Black Conch men roamed; their women stayed still. That was a rule, even for a woman like Miss Rain. She dared not ask him to stay; she had the wrong credentials. Planter's progeny. He was sleeping with the enemy. That was the unspoken secret of their attraction and the reason for his leaving, too.

Life rose and wrapped a towel around his waist. Dawn light was pouring through the blinds. She lay on one side and watched him.

"Damn you," she said.

He was looking for his drawers. He turned.

"Damn me?"

He came and sat down by her side, rested one hand on her hip, which was covered by the sheet.

"What?"

"Nothing."

He looked down at her with that long-jawed face of his. Full of his sense of self, of being himself and being alone.

"What? Say it."

"Say what?"

"Say the thing."

Now she was annoyed. She turned over and gave him her back.

He watched her and steupsed. He stroked his throat and thought about pushing her off the bed. Argument brewing already, and he was only two days here.

He got up and pulled on his drawers. He hadn't brought too many clothes with him. He'd stayed longer than he'd planned. Getting there had been his only plan. Not staying. And not going back either. He went back to the bed and sat down. This woman confused the hell out of him.

"Are you confused?" he said.

She didn't turn round.

"Ay," he said. He slapped her rump. "I'm asking you. Are you confused?"

He saw her body start to heave, with laughter.

"No."

"I don't have a clean jersey," he said.

"That's not my problem," she replied, her back still to him.

"Ayy, Miss Lady. My drawers need a wash too. Can I give them to the servants?"

She turned around and glared.

"I'm joking."

She crossed her arms behind her head and gazed up at the ceiling. Never had she felt so stuck.

"I know what you must be thinking."

"Oh yeah?"

"Yeah."

"What am I thinking?"

"Am I staying?"

She narrowed her eyes.

He grinned.

"I don't have any servants here," she said. "Only Geoffrey who tends the garden. And Phillipa, who comes once a week to mop the floors. There's a washing machine in the kitchen. You can pelt your clothes in there."

"Do you want me to stay?"

"No."

He shook his head.

"I was fine without you. We were both fine without you. You can leave when you are ready."

Life felt sad at this. Woman could bouf man bad, bad. This was how the women of Black Conch were: bad.

He got up and prepared himself to say something that needed saying, but he had no idea what it was. All the sexing had muddled his head. His feelings for her had ambushed him. His son Reggie was a second ambush. Then there was that mermaid, too. It had all rushed at him and now he had on a pair of two-day-old drawers and no friggin clean jersey.

"I love you and you know that," he said, pointing his finger right at her, as if she were a target. "But I cannot stay here," and he jerked his thumb upwards to the ceiling, "in this house. Not here. You know?"

Miss Rain did know. This had all come up before: she couldn't leave the house and he would never stay in it. She couldn't abandon the estate, the house, the land, the property. He had asked her once. His idea had been to live in the forest, or go to Port Isabella, start again. She had refused. That was why he'd left. She had refused him many times. What had he to offer? Nothing, except a power she had vastly underestimated. Eventually, he had just disappeared; no note. He didn't need to leave one.

"I ent no house nigga."

They stared at each other. The word was like a wrecking ball. The shame of it was her shame, always. His fury.

"I never invited you to stay here in this house with me."

He nodded. He knew he could hurt her whenever he wanted, but when he did it, he also felt pain. Loving a white woman was his life's torment.

"And don't give me that 'you're free to go' speech either," he said. "I cyan stay anywhere else in this damn village because you own all the other houses too. This entire goddamn part of the island belongs to you."

Arcadia flinched. None of this seemed to matter when they were children.

"Can't you stay because of your son?"

"I'll stay because I want to. If I want to. Because this is my hometown, even if you own it. I grew up here . . . It's not the best situation for a man like me. I never wanted it."

"I've sold off plenty land since you left. Given it away for next to nothing. Plenty places I don't own now. Many people farm, own their own homes. I saw to that. I hardly collect the rent. You make me feel like I screwing everyone bad."

Life pressed a palm to his chest. An ancient pride; he would not be torn down by 'Miss Rain' and her type. It was a curse, loving her. Many times he had wished otherwise. Once, as a boy, he even thought about cutting his heart out of his chest with a penknife.

"Live where you want." She had tears in her eyes. "It's not my fault, this whole goddamn situation. I don't need to love you, either. Go."

She got out of bed, naked, and searched around for her underwear and shoes. Her backside was dimpled and tears streamed down her face. In this mood she might punch him.

He sat down on the bed again and raised his head to the ceiling, to the sky above, and then to the whole damn universe.

"Okay," he said.

She found a clean cotton panty from the dresser and put them on, then her shoes which were under a rocking chair—cork-soled sandals, with a T-bar. She stood staring at him, in her panty and shoes, and said, "We can do better than this."

He looked her way. "This?"

"History or love. One must win. I cannot fight history. I cannot. You win. I'm bad. I always will be. But we can do better than letting history win out over love."

She was pulling on a dress, the same one she'd worn yesterday. Mauve, pretty. When her head surfaced through the neck she pulled one of her casual-stern faces, a face which said this dress still fits, but only just; a face which said I'm trying to stay calm; a face which said, you see this master-slave thing? I done with it. Is a big thing, hard thing for us, and we gonna talk this through for good and all.

"Come on," she said. "Let's have some breakfast."

David Baptiste's journal, January 2016

We were sitting there, she and I, in the cold cells in the basement of the police station in late August 1976, facing each other but not watching each other. Aycayia was weeping. She was turning back to mermaid in front my eyes. Like the shock of her second kidnapping speed up the change. I fraid for her. I understood their plot, to call the Yankee men back so they could take her God knows where, a zoo? Porthos and Priscilla had been keeping the whole thing quiet. All morning I shouted for help, but the cells were down in the basement for a good reason. No windows, no light coming in; no one could hear me. At midday Porthos came down with a jug of water, cups, a loaf of bread and a jar of peanut butter. He wouldn't catch my eye. I demanded he let us go, pleaded with him to see that what he doing was wrong. But his mind was already made up. He tell me they called them Yankee men and they were coming soon to take her back. I ask him where they taking her and he say is not his or my business.

Aycayia was curled up on the thin bunk bed, her back to us. She had gone inside herself and stopped talking.

I beg him to let us go, telling him I would put her back in the sea where we first meet, but he only stare at her. We could both see a dorsal fin coming, all up her spine.

"Let her go," I begged him, but he stared at me like he don't know himself or what to do. He look afraid and unsure of heself.

"Meet?" he say, and I saw his jaw flinch. To this day I remember his words and my reply.

"Dis some kind of love affair? You been fuckin a fish?" And he laughed loudly and with contempt and this rile up my blood to say, "And you fuck that damn, hard-faced, bad-minded bitch?"

We glared at each other for a few moments, kind of dumbstruck, beyond words. He leave the plate of bread and the jug next to my cell so I could reach it, lock the door and then we were alone again. Aycayia was curled up in a ball; she was never going to be the same again, the woman I wanted to marry and live with. All of that some damn, stupid fantasy. I got carried away with myself. It dawned on me she wasn't for this world; she was another thing, altogether; a ban had been put on her head, damnation for eternity. Her real jail was the sea. I had put on her all kind of man dreams. By the time them Yankee men arrived they would find what they were looking for and had left behind here, in Black Conch, months back, a rare and beautiful creature, a mermaid.

That afternoon, Life and Miss Rain got to know of the arrest from Ce-Ce, who had heard it from a neighbour, who'd heard the sounds of the raid, seen David's house was empty. They flew down there in the jeep, found both doors broken in, a chair turned over, a broken plate on the floor. Reggie, who was with them, cried when he realised his friend had been stolen away. They went back to the big house in a sombre mood. She had to be rescued.

"Porthos came to see me the other day," Arcadia said. "You two were somewhere else. I should have stopped them, then."

"Them?"

"Porthos and Priscilla."

"They came here?"

"Yes."

"Those two fools. Still as bad as each other."

"You know them?"

"Of course. That man Porthos lazy and stupid. A gambler too. Thiefing money and selling anything he can, on the side—or that was the case when I last lived in these parts. And that Priscilla woman vex no ass—all the time making trouble for everyone."

"Her sons were on the boat, when she was caught, or so I hear from David. They identified her. Aycayia had started to walk around the village. Only a matter of time."

Arcadia was remembering Priscilla's curse. People could think bad thoughts, say bad things. Next thing, bad things happened.

Reggie signed that he was scared.

Miss Rain interpreted this.

"Doh worry, son," Life told him. "She will be back here, in this house, by the end of today. Safe."

In the dead of night, under a full and waxing moon, Life and Miss Rain drove to Small Rock, taking with them the Barracuda, a pair of bolt-cutters, some rope, and a torch. The station was dark, closed up, one guard on duty, asleep on a chair in front of the door to the basement cells. Life put the cold nose of the gun to the guard's temple and sooted him as a wake-up call. The man's eyes flew open and he reached for his gun, which Life had already taken. He stooped close to the man's face and put one finger to his lips and said, "Quiet, now."

Miss Rain said, "Put your goddamn hands behind your back." The man complied, a man who'd never before had to guard any-thing important in his life. It all happened in seconds. Miss Rain pointed both guns while Life lashed the man's hands with the rope, gagged his mouth, tied his feet and took the keys to the basement.

There, also asleep on a chair, was Superintendent Porthos John. His gun was on his lap. They were on him in an instant, relieving him of his weapon, switching on the light. "Hands in the air," Life shouted, aiming his gun at the balls of the police officer, a man who owed him money from way back, a man with whom he had old scores to settle. "Up," he said. "Don't move a muscle."

10

Huracan

≋

NEXT MORNING, SIX AM, THE SKIES WERE PINK. The howlers sounded as though the mountains were arguing. Flocks of turquoise and yellow parakeets fluttered from the forest canopy and headed south. One by one, the peacocks in the garden trotted into the house, to roost. When Miss Rain clapped to shoo one out, it dodged her and trotted straight back. She stood on the porch in her dressing gown and watched the sea. She could see the grey swells forming far out, full of an indolent power, and knew what was happening. Rip currents were forcing the sea apart in places. She shuddered and went back inside. David was at the breakfast table with a cup of fresh coffee, deep in thought.

"Storm brewing," she said.

"I think she's dying."

"No, David."

"I doh think she'll make it. Not this time. She doh want to live, doh want to go back to mermaid. She go drown sheself if we put she back."

Miss Rain sat down in the chair opposite him. "Where is she?"

"I carried her to the bathtub, last night. After allyuh went to sleep. Her tail coming back. She cyan walk again."

"No."

"Is the shock of her kidnap."

Miss Rain wanted to weep.

"I love her."

"I know, and me too, and Reggie. Even Life is in a kinda shock." Life had taken Porthos to an abandoned shack he knew of nearby, bound up like a crab. They would keep him out the way, till they released her back into the sea. Like Reggie, Life was still asleep. Reggie had no idea Aycayia was hiding in the house.

"We can't let them Yankee men take her back," said David.

"Best I can do is keep them off my land, for a short time."

David was glassy-eyed. "She tried to kill herself."

"No."

"Yes. I found her hanging . . . day before yesterday, from that big old fig tree in the forest, like she knew that was how to stop this. She doh want to go back. To being so lonely."

"I'm so sorry, David."

"I shouldn' have cut her down."

"Look, storm coming now, and her tail coming back. Now is a good chance for she to . . . disappear. Yankee men won't chase her in a storm. The village men will bring their boats in. No one will go out. But they done reach by now from Miami."

"Where is Porthos?"

"Life take care of him. For now. So we have some time."

"Time?"

"To think. Not much, but breathing time. Time to hatch a plan."

"Plan? What plan? To put her back?"

"Isn't that what you were going to do, anyway?"

David had to admit this had been his first intention, months ago, to put her straight back into the sea.

"That was a good plan."

David gazed into a space in front of him. A tear spilled down his cheek.

"Why women hate other women so? Eh?"

"David, we a long way from knowing that."

"Is because we play them bad? Is man fault women treat each other bad? Is we who run them down. We doh like to stay home, mind children. Men bad, so women bad too?"

"No, David. Sometimes people just have a malicious temperament. No one to blame but themselves."

"I tired of games."

"Yeah, and me."

"That mermaid woman is first time I see clearly how to be a man. How to be myself, behave well. Is like she teach me how to be on the right side of good. You can't play games with she. She so innocent."

Miss Rain nodded. "Sometimes, we women not fair even in our own thoughts about ourselves. You men born from us, and yet you assume power. Is we who give you that power. You see that man, Life? That man make me wait, make me patient."

"I know."

"'Love' isn't a good enough word to describe what I feel for Life."

"Is he staying?"

She shrugged.

"You deserve happiness."

She laughed, "Life doh make me 'happy,' he does make me vexed half the time. Reggie and I are cool, so far. Is like now,

today, is the next instalment between me and Life. Every day is
a surprise. Reggie needs him more than I do."

David knew this was a lie.

"Life is a damn fool if he leave again."

They looked at one another, both heartsick, on tenterhooks.

"Is she talking?"

"She hasn't said much in a few days now."

"Is she eating?"

He shook his head.

"Okay. I'll go up."

Upstairs, in the pink-tiled bathroom, in the old pink bathtub,
Aycayia was sleeping. Her small chest rose and fell as she dreamt.
She was sitting upright, slumped against the wall. There were no
mirrors in the room, and Miss Rain was thankful for that. She
could see by the sealed-up stump of her lower half that Aycayia
was being re-trapped. Virgin and sweet voice, men had been
drawn to look, to lose themselves, just as David had. Reggie too.
Her tattoos of suns, moons, fish and birds, faded though they
were, spoke of how her people made little distinction between
human and animal, of how, as a young woman, she had been
cursed to cross the slight boundary between them, to be alone,
her only companion an old crone turned into a leatherback. Old
woman, pretty woman, both rejects. Womanhood was a dangerous business if you didn't get it right.

Miss Rain went closer and stooped by the tub.

"Ayyy," she whispered.

Aycayia woke with a start. Her face was sombre. Tears fell and
her eyes were fierce silver stars. She grasped at Miss Rain, threw
her arms around her neck.

"Shhh, dou dou, shh."

Aycayia wailed and said, "Home," again and again. Miss Rain held her as best she could, but in truth she, too, was distraught at the thought of her re-banishment.

After some minutes, Miss Rain dabbed Aycayia's cheeks with a towel and said, softly, "Will you eat something?"

Aycayia shook her head.

"You are safe here with us."

"I not safe, ever."

"Yes, you are safe here."

She shook her head.

"A storm is coming."

She nodded. "To take me away."

Aycayia looked down at what was once her legs. Her tail would grow big big, another few metres at least, a magnificent apparition. When she was mermaid again she would be very powerful; and it was coming.

"I need to go back to the sea," she said.

"I know."

"Will you take me?"

"If you want me to."

"Will David take me?"

"Yes."

"When?"

"When it's right. When you want."

"I will miss you." Her face trembled. "I must go back. Women curse win. I will go back, swim, swim."

"We will see you again, though."

Aycayia shot her a sharp stare and nodded. "Yes." And then she started to sing, high and low, soft and strong, there in the bathtub in the great house dripping with lace. The sound of her voice, sweet and melancholy, echoed all morning through the house, as the winds picked up and careened in from the east, as the gangs of howlers chorused in fractious disharmony, as the parakeets rose up and flocked south, as the ocean rose and swelled further out.

By lunchtime, winds were thirty-five miles per hour. The radio announced the storm; a hurricane, then category 4, was brewing far out and it was aiming itself directly at the island. Usually they struck further north. Usually, they bisected the island chain, around about Barbados—that, or they scooted into the Caribbean basin and demolished Jamaica, or Haiti, mashing up all in their wake, decapitating buildings, uprooting trees, snatching up cars, farm animals, demolishing schools, hospitals, entire neighbourhoods, flooding land, crops, cities, drowning shacks and shanties. Hurricane was a helluva thing. They arrived this time of year and though they sometimes didn't hit land, and sometimes blew themselves out, not this one. Rosamund, it was called, and it was heading straight for the island of Black Conch.

David Baptiste's journal, February 2016

I hardly know what to say about the time of Rosamund, 1976. Still just about the most devastating storm ever to hit Black Conch. Fifteen years, at least, we ent see a storm like it. That time it was because of the mermaid. I'm sure of that. It came to claim her back. All during that time in the howling of the winds, I could hear those women laughing. I can still hear them from time to time, like they enter my head, long ago, and I cyan shake them out. The foreshore of St. Constance was sheltered by the back of the mountain range, but the slopes themselves were hit, the forest, the ancient trees, the village itself, much of what was on the flat. For two days the winds blew and rain fell hard; we were sitting ducks. You cyan move an island out of the way of a storm. Some people leave and drive south, others boarded-over windows best they could. A storm was inside me too, over the loss of my heart-mate. She lived with me five whole months. The time of her changing back into a young woman was like a magic time, full of getting to know her and myself. Like I forget how we meet, in the sea, by those jagged rocks; I forget about what she was when I saved her from the jetty. Over those months, I forget the fish part.

The night we were in jail, when I was watching she turning back, her spine bringing up a dorsal fin, scales shining on her flesh, only then I remember what she'd been. Bad things can happen if you say bad things; I know that now.

Myself and Life went down to the seafront. Waves were rolling in, rain coming down. Like a war coming. The boats were pitching around and anchor chains would bust. It was too rough to swim out to the boat. A fella we knew from the village was helping people in an old taxi boat, a zodiac dinghy. We climbed in and sped out to *Simplicity*, which was already fulling with water. It take some skill to ride the swells and drag her up onto land, up behind the line of sea almond trees. We bring her in as far as we could, all the time knowing that we might have to take the boat out again, to put she back.

Every man jack bring his boat in. The bay was empty but for big dark waves. Ce-Ce was still serving rum and a lot of men gathered in there. That's when I saw them Yankee men again, both of them, drinking a rum, around midday before the storm hit us. My blood turn to ice at the sight of them. They were sitting quiet quiet at a table, the old white man and his son. No tourists arrive that time of year; the place different then. August is wet season, hurricane season start.

Life asked if that was them.

I nodded.

A man who loves a woman enough can do the right thing. That's when I knew how much Life love Miss Rain. He already done spring me and the mermaid from jail; next thing he move in on those men, cool so. Life is a Mandingo warrior-type black man, the kind white people fraid. He only have to set up his face to frighten them away. He have a way about him, a confidence from how he think; this time he didn't act no part; it was too easy to frighten them fellers.

"Can I join you?" he said, sitting down before they say no.

The younger one begin to turn even more white.

"David." He motion to me. "Bring up a seat."

I sat down too, so we had them cornered. Behind them is only rain. In front of them only us.

Life ask them direct what were they doing in Black Conch. He was chewing on a matchstick. He watch them real curious.

The old man say is none of our goddamn business. He tell us to leave them alone.

Life's eyebrows shoot up. "Alone?" he say.

"Shoo, move away," the old man repeated.

"Shoo?" Life say, cool.

"Leave us in peace. We are here on some business."

"What kind of shoo business is this?" Life asked.

The old man set his cap straight and glared at Life, like he might even take him outside if it wasn't raining so much. Old man does be bad, sometimes; doh fuck with no old man, in truth.

Life laughed. He picked at his teeth. He look at the old man and then his stupid-ass son and say out straight, "You still looking for that mermaid, again, or what?"

The old man's face screwed up and he say something that sound like a cuss word, but still Life play him real cool.

"David," he say to me, "tell him. Tell him bout how you save that poor woman, how is you who cut she down, rescue her."

I swear those white men almost fainted.

Life smiled big and slow. "Tell them, nuh."

"It was you?" stammered the old man. "You stole our mer-maid?"

Boy, even now, just the thought of them makes my blood turn to hot and I said, proud, "Yes, I cut her down."

"You goddamn mutherfucker!" the old man shouted. "You stole our property. I'll have you arrested again. Locked up for good."

I woulda cuff the old man to the ground if Life ent stop me.

Ce-Ce was behind the bar. She give a look to one of her sons to say get them out before she kill them. I ent go lie, that younger man look ready to shit his pants.

Life raised his hand, as if to say no one move, no one run them out, no one kill them. Life was playing the long game. That is why I know how much he love Miss Rain; he not so bound up with Aycayia, he more able to use his mind, more able to play chess with them fellas. He doing it out of love, for the woman he love and for his son.

"David," he say, "tell these gentlemen your story."

And so I try, best I could, to tell them how she change back, how she tail fall off before I can put her back in the sea, how she begin to walk and how Miss Rain teach she Black Conch lan-guage and how she start to settle back in, how she was able to read the skies, talk to trees, know how to make cassava bread. How she came from Cuba, and how she was cursed by her sistren, long ago.

But I ent tell them about the marriage part, or about how she try to hang sheself from the giant fig tree. I ent tell them about the fish rain.

The old man listened but like he wasn't ready to hear anything. Like he was only waiting for me to finish.

"I don't give a damn flying rat's ass about no goddamn curse from wherever the fuck you say she come from. I don't care if she came from Cuba, Venezuela, or from Timbuktu. I don't care if she could walk, talk, play the violin or do the hula. Okay?"

We stared at him, shocked.

"Skip it all. Nice story. Boo hoo," he mocked us. Then he repeated that she was theirs. They caught her, with the licence they bought, right there from the bar, to fish in these waters and keep what they caught. They were taking her back to Miami, that same day.

When I stammered out, "But she's human," the old man slammed his hand on the table. "No, she isn't human at all. Not last time I heard. Last time I heard, she was turning back to what she was."

Man could murder man. I could have murdered that old man with my own hands, there and then. Life held me back; he was still playing them best he could.

Life said she was not for them to capture again, for them to take away, and keep or sell. That set the old man off damning us all to hell and back. He hoped the storm would blow us all away. What's his was his, caught fair and square. He could do what he damn well pleased.

Everybody saw what happened next. Priscilla appeared with Porthos, and this time Porthos truly vexed from being locked up.

Priscilla had gone looking for him, heard him bawling and let him out. He strode straight up to the men who were quarrelling, took out his gun and shot it into the air. The bullet went up into the roof, the hole much remarked upon to this day, and when Ce-Ce ready to tell stories, she will talk of that day when all of them big men arguing about a damn mermaid, when hurricane Rosamund was on its way.

"You," Porthos said to Life, "you are under arrest."

Life didn't move a damn muscle, he did not flinch, for he had something to say to Porthos he hadn't said yet.

"Me?"

"Yes. Right now."

"For what?"

"For what? Are you mad?" Priscilla stepped in. "For kidnapping a policeman. For breaking into a police barracks, for aiding and abetting a man who tief a mermaid, for . . ." And she stopped and she looked as if she go strangle Life.

"Ayy." Life got up from his chair. He then showed how bad he could be.

"I the tief? I tiefing what? A mermaid? This man is the goddamn tief," he said, pointing at Porthos. "This man owe me money, five hundred dollars at least. He owe every goddamn man in Small Rock money and he been thiefing the damn police force blind, stealing anything and everything he could, since from day one. Money, tools, clothes, old uniforms, selling them off to bandits and whoever; old vehicles, selling them to people on Port Isabella. He have more than one racket going on the side. He passing this and that, here and there. It have a word. Profiteering. This man sell he own grandmother to anyone who would buy. You de damn focking thief," Life said to Porthos, and he spat his matchstick on the ground. He looked around and everyone in Ce-Ce's was dead quiet. Ce-Ce nodded and clicked her throat.

Everyone stared at Porthos.

"That is slander," Priscilla said.

"That is the damn truth. Man stealing the force blind and everyone else around too. And now he want to make big bucks with these damn white assholes and their damn mermaid which they 'caught' and want to sell."

"I am not an asshole," said the old Yankee man. "Take that back."

"Shut up," said Porthos. He pointed his gun at Life and pulled back the catch on the trigger. "I will shoot your damn black ass if you say one more word."

"No," shouted David. "Doh shoot no one. Is that damn woman Priscilla who cause all of this. *She* is the troublemaker here."

"Me?"

"Yes, you and your bad mind. Wherever you is, it have trouble. Trouble is your speciality. All you can do is maco other people business and hurt them. You is one damn macotious bitch. Is it true Short Leg is his son?"

Priscilla stared.

"What?" said Porthos, and he lowered his gun.

"You fucking blind?" said David. "When everyone can see he have the same face as you. He just a smaller version of you, except he have one short leg. You and this woman done brushing each other for years, and you telling me you ent have at least one chile from she?"

"Baptiste, shut your fuckin' mouth," said Priscilla.

"What, Short Leg is my son?"

Priscilla stood, hands on hips, and gave David a look from hell.

"And the two of you gonna do what? Charge these stupid

men a big ransom? Some kind of fine? Split the money? Half and half?"

"He's my son? Eh, woman?" Porthos looked furious.

"Shut up," fumed Priscilla.

"Why you never tell me?"

"Fuck you, Baptiste," Priscilla said, her voice dead in her throat.

"Woman, tell me is a lie."

Well the whole damn bar riveted to the spot. Priscilla looked around, at everyone, all the people she knew from birth. Truth is, she had planned to use the ransom money to get the hell away from this small place; take her sons, go elsewhere, start again, where no one knew her.

"Is no lie."

The old Yankee man stood and shouted, "For Christ sakes, can someone arrest this man, Life, or whatever his goddamn name is. You people and your goddamn stupid names."

"Shut up," said Porthos.

Next thing that happened was no joke. Everyone in Ce-Ce's heard it.

The rain stop.

The winds dropped.

Then, all around. Voices, quiet quiet.

Laughing, women laughing.

Then, a tear in the sky, like a big brown paper bag ripped open.

Things began to land on the pavement and the roof and they could all hear the sound of hard-soft thumps. Everyone looked out the windows and people rose from their chairs to check if their eyes saw right.

Jellyfish, man o' war, falling from the sky, suspended like in

Jell-O, and then hitting the ground. Like the ocean tipped upside down from a bucket. Starfish, jellyfish, octopus . . . all manner of sea creatures were falling from some kind of hole in the sky.

"Is Rosamund," said one woman. "She pelting us with fish."

"Is de damn hurricane," said another. "Taking up fish from the sea further east. It coming now."

"Holy fucking Moses," whispered Thomas Clayson, the old white man from Florida, a banker, a golfer, a bridge player, husband and a father, bad at everything he ever did. He could not love; he could not make anyone love him back. That had been his problem in life. He had chosen wrong, and had nothing but rotten luck, always. He did not love his son or his wife enough. He had known that to return to Black Conch would be a long shot. But he'd done nothing but dream of the mermaid all these months, her long black hair blossoming around her, beneath the boat, that deep satisfying wump into her flanks, with the gaff, steel in meat. He could still feel it in his balls. Still see her hate-filled eyes, and remember his desire to piss all over her. Night after night he had dreamt of that bitch mermaid. She had swum through his dreams back in Florida. She had haunted him. Even his wife had noticed he had been sleeping badly, and she slept in another room. And his son, his sissy-assed poetry-reading son hadn't been the same either. They had done the opposite of "bonding," man to man, since that ill-fated fishing trip back in April. Goddamn village of Black Conch, goddamn backwards fishermen and their kin, all married to each other, all interrelated and backwards and lying and cheating each other. And now this: it was raining fucking sea creatures. He wouldn't leave. He was going nowhere till he got what he came for. He had papers to prove she belonged to him. He wasn't leaving the island again without the mermaid.

II

Rosamund

≋

Curse came back
Rosamund her name
Why huracan get woman's name?
Rosamund came to take me back to sea
Heart feeling in my chest
would come to the sea with me
I feel it even now
long time later

Sitting in a bathtub
tail grew back again
Part of me came back to me
fish woman

Do not be sad

I could have grown to be a woman too
and curse other women
Use bad thoughts

I am not sad
I am not lonely too much this time
I think of my friends in Black Conch
Huracan
take me away
Gone gone gone beyond gone
David? I saw him again many times
every year, for nearly 40 cycles

———

David Baptiste's journal, February 2016

Later that day the winds got stronger. The clouds were thick and black as iron and the rain was heavy. Water poured down the hill and flooded the streets. Waves were up to ten metres out in the bay. The radio tell us the storm only twenty-four hours away from landfall. Trees swayed in the hills like I see only once before—the hurricane in 1961, when I was a little youth. I forget what a hurricane can do, how it feel when it coming. Is like a fury come upon us. And yes, I wonder if it coming for she alone. Once upon a time, there was a young woman, and a big storm carried her away to sea; second upon a time, there was a young woman and a big storm came to carry she back to the sea. That's what she tell me. That her life had to play a certain way, no change from the ol'-time legend.

Me and Life went back to Miss Rain's house. It was raining so hard, windscreen wipers only wiping water around. Panic in the air, panic in my nerves. No one else was driving around in that kind of weather. We figure we go back up to the big house and hole up for a time. We left Porthos and his woman to talk about their newfound son, and we left the ol white man and his everyday son down there too, all of them getting drunk.

Well, I never ketch such a fright as when we arrived back. Reggie and Miss Rain were upstairs with Aycayia. Everything had come back. She was like when I first rescued her all them months back at my home, in the old tub I found in the yard. Her tail had grown back. Helluva thing. We could see her now as half fish, or some huge game animal, and we could see why the old white man was so crazy to find her again. This was what they remembered, one big mudderass mermaid: long tail, silver-black and patterned like a barracuda or a shark, skin glittering, hands back to fins. Her face had changed back too, back to mermaid face, teeth back to real sharp, eyes bright, more wildness in how she look at us. She frightened me. Imagine that. My one true love . . . She make me ketch myself.

She was singing. Miss Rain was sitting next to her on a chair; Reggie was on the floor. The three of them look like some kind of funeral happening. The mermaid, like she singing a lonesome "Ave Maria" for her own self death. She was making hand signs to Reggie. Life was shocked. This is what we been hiding all along. He ketch himself real good, too. "Holy Jesus," he said.

Miss Rain nodded. Reggie was in tears. Mermaid sang for herself, her lonesome self, and she was singing for us too.

Three of us went down to the kitchen to talk and make a plan. Reggie stayed upstairs with her. All of us was in shock. Miss Rain was in tears. Life open a bottle of Vat 19 and pour himself a good shot. I took one too. I feel a terrible sorrow coming for me with those winds.

Miss Rain asked what we should do, and Life said is now we

have to put her back, or we have to wait till after the storm. Miss Rain said we had to wait, that we couldn't take Aycayia out in the pirogue for at least another day.

I remind them that the white men were still here in Black Conch, and they all now looking for her. They only seeing dollar bills, and they figure they have paperwork to own her, take she back. I asked what we would do if they came up here with more police and find her, because Porthos John would back them up. He was in on it too, and after the storm they could come and take her by force. I was scared for her. We didn't have any time left for her to live with us here. A handful of friends was not enough to protect her. Then I had an idea. What if we didn't take her so far? I explained how we could drive her down to the seafront, that night. Late. How we could back my truck onto the jetty; we could carry her in a tarp, all of us. Drop her in the sea, right there. Then she could slip away.

Life poured himself another shot of rum and Miss Rain told him to give her some.

Nerves were boiling up in my stomach. I never believed this could happen, that she have to go back to the ocean, back to who she was.

Life looked at me and then at Miss Rain. All of us drank a shot of rum.

"Sounds like a plan," said Life.

So, at midnight, only hours before Rosamund struck, they went down to the foreshore. Reggie went too. He wouldn't stay home alone in the old house. The peacocks were all inside, terrified, nesting under the kitchen table. The pot hounds were hiding under Miss Rain's bed. Reggie couldn't hear the shrieking winds, but he saw the trees bending backwards, the jalousies banging shut, the blackened skies at lunchtime. He was adamant he would accompany them, to say goodbye to his first and only friend. Aycayia lay wrapped in tarpaulin in the back of David's truck, singing songs of loss, for the loss of her people and the loss of her own innocence here on earth. She was no longer locked out of the secrets of womanhood. She was going back, same, but different. She sang for this bereavement, which was also a kind of victory, one she would think about for an eternity. In some way, she had beaten the women's curse.

The hill between Miss Rain's house and the village was steep and winding. They inched along, David driving into the wind. No one spoke. They could just hear Aycayia singing, a sound like Africa, like the Andes, like old Creole hymnals, like shamanic icaros from a time when people healed themselves with simple herbal wisdom, when they understood all the kingdoms of the earth.

"My God," whispered Miss Rain.

Life reached to hold her hand.

"It's beautiful."

They stopped at the curve of the hill, peered hard into the night and saw mountainous waves in the ocean, breaking hard with rough spray meeting spray. Walls of sea.

"Shit," said Miss Rain.

David inched the truck forward. At the bend in the road they took the right-hand fork to the foreshore. Waves were coming over the road. The light on the jetty glowed orange and showed the narrow strip of concrete buffeted by waves. This was their only chance. Now or never.

They crawled along towards the jetty.

Above them, in the guesthouse on the hill above Ce-Ce's, Thomas Clayson and his son Hank were getting drunk. They sat at a table with a bottle of puncheon rum between them.

"I came back too late," Thomas Clayson said. "Too damn late."

Hank had thought a lot in the past months about the woman they'd pulled from the sea—he had penned sonnets to her, he had seen something he never thought he would see. A hybrid of mythical dimensions, a creature only told of in stories. But she was true! She was the result of the powers of an ancient goddess, Jagua. He had done some research, found the old legend in a study of the folktales and myths of the region. It was only a stray paragraph, but it mentioned a mermaid called Aycayia. She had been banished to the sea because of her irksome beauty. So it turned out she wasn't just a story. He'd flown back with his father in the hope that he might see her again, but also vowing that if his father tried to capture her, he would stop him. That was the reason he was here, in the middle of a hurricane, in the hellhole of Black Conch, during his final term at law school. His father had gone mad. His parents were finally breaking up and he was glad of it. The mermaid had been the last straw. When his mother told him, confidentially, that she was leaving, "escaping" was the word she'd used.

Hank Clayson had been thinking hard about how to play decoy, to hamper his father's attempts to recapture the unfortunate creature. He had a hunch, after the scene in the rum shop that day, that the men in the village knew where she was.

"Dad," he said. "Maybe she's just not yours to keep."

"Keep? What? She's mine. Maybe . . ." And Thomas Clayson,

flushed from the 100 proof rum—the kind of spirit that can fuel a cigarette lighter, strip silver, catch fire—gave his son a withering look. "Maybe you just don't like . . ."

"What, Dad? Mermaids?"

"No."

"Then what, Dad?"

His father struck the table with the empty glass and wiped his lips with his sleeve.

"Women."

Hank was twenty-one. He was coming to be quite handsome; he loved many things: his mother, books, poetry, friends, cherry ice cream, fresh tomatoes, Miles Davis, the Ramones, autumn, the mermaid, and yes, women, girls, their legs, their smiles, their shyness and their toughness and yes, also, yes, yes . . . other men.

"Maybe I like what I like, Dad," he said.

His father's eyes rolled backwards into his head. "Maybe you and your mother can go to hell," he slurred, and then slumped over onto the table.

The truck inched backwards along the jetty as the surf rose and crashed against the windows. Aycayia had stopped singing. David managed to position the truck most of the way down the jetty; the end was so badly buffeted by waves that it was lost in spray. Life and David hopped out of the truck and Miss Rain and Reggie climbed up into the tray. Lashing rain. The sound of women laughing rattled through the winds. The mermaid was still, looking up at them, especially Reggie. She made signs with her hands. Her tail and skin had gone darker, black like ink, and she glistened, as though in camouflage with the skies and the sea. Her face was streaked with tears. She was radiant in her sorrow, for her impending exile, for what she was about to lose again. They began to tug at the tarpaulin she was resting on, and then the tarp came away from the truck and became a kind of hammock. They hauled it to the edge of the jetty. It was there, next to the raging sea, on the same jetty where he'd first seen her crucified, and rescued her, David said goodbye. They clung to one another and David whispered in her ear, *Meet me again, sweet love. Meet me again where we met, at those rocks, same place, same time, next year. I will see you there, I will see you again, dear friend.* They embraced and then she slipped from the tarp into the sea, vanishing in a moment into the crashing waves.

David Baptiste's journal, February 2016

We hurried back to the house, rain drowning out words and thoughts, my chest pounding with rage like I'd never known before. The punishment for her was for me too. And for Reggie, poor fella. I never saw him look so forlorn. Love for another person, even one so pure, have its rules and its rule-makers. People does like to mash up other people; woman does envy other woman; man does treat woman bad. I drove up the hill that night with bad feelings in my heart. I hoped she would hear my words, that I would see her again, once the storm pass, once some time pass too.

When we arrived back up the hill, we knew the storm was just hours away. I didn't try to get back to my own house; I ent been there since Porthos came with his men to kidnap us. I was sure it would get blown away. Miss Rain's house had a large basement. Soon as we got back we started to take mattresses and bedding and hurricane lamps and food down there; we took the dogs down there and we even take them damn peacocks, all six of them. All life in the house went downstairs, to where it was safe. Must be around two in the morning when we all get pack up down there. None of us talked about the mermaid, though I guess all of us were thinking about her. Hell coming for us, hell taking her away. I knew my life would never be the same. I was twenty-six years old, and yet I knew that the first part of my life had ended. Next day, everything would be different. I was right about that.

Rosamund hit the north coast of Black Conch the next morning, at approximately six am, on the twenty-seventh of August, 1976. Records have it that it was, and still is, the worst storm of the late twentieth century to devastate one of the Lesser Antilles, a direct hit. David, Reggie, Life, Miss Rain and her pot hounds and the peacocks were all in the basement of the great house. Winds were up to a hundred and eighty-five miles an hour, a category 5 storm. They razored flat the trees in the hills. Mahogany came down, old cyp trees came down, all the old bois canot in the forest were levelled in a matter of minutes. Even the giant fig broke in half. The winds sounded like a herd of wild horses thundering in. They could hear the house loosen itself from its foundations. The old boards didn't stand a chance. Over a hundred years old, they splintered and broke, flying away with the winds. Shutters flew away, whole. Roof tiles flew up and swirled into a clatter of shale. Each of those tiles had been hand-nailed into the roof timbers. Obliterated by the storm that had come for the mermaid, they spiralled into a vast vortex of debris. This was Guabancex herself, Casike of the Winds, rotating her arms, unfurling her rage.

For more than an hour the huracan lashed them, before the eye was upon them. The quiet was more terrifying than the winds.

"Listen," said Life. But there was nothing to hear. Miss Rain hugged Reggie tight. The mermaid, Aycayia, was already miles away, heading north.

"Listen."

No winds. And no more laughter. A dead lull. Like the heartbeat of a human soul had been silenced.

The pores in Miss Rain's arms rose up. She crossed herself and muttered under her breath the only prayer she knew: *Hail Mary full of grace* . . .

Reggie wept in her arms.

The silence lasted for twenty minutes or so, as the eye passed over them, a gaping hole.

Life knew then, in those minutes of quiet, that he wanted to stay here, with his family, his woman and his son, that he would never leave them again. David knew he would be a lonely man, forever gazing out to sea, searching for Aycayia. Miss Rain knew that her home was decimated and she felt a certain relief. She knew that she wouldn't rebuild. She would move, find another place to settle, nearby. The storm was sweeping things away in its path; that was its grand design, its meaning for them all. She would sell off as much land as she could, give it away, even; all she wanted was to be left alive, in peace. Reggie clung to his mother's bosom. He'd never known so many things happen so quickly: a friend, a father and then this storm. When the eye passed and more winds came, blowing more of the great house away, and blowing more trees down, and flattening more houses in the hills, they all sat quiet; quiet in themselves, all of them waiting. Life went to Arcadia and hugged her tight and hugged his son tight too and he rubbed his chin and thought of the mermaid, how her life had affected his, and how she had shown him how to be brave. Everything had changed up in Black Conch and he'd never expected that. Some places stay same same, never change. Not here. Not in this tip of an island jooking out into the sea, not in a place full of the ghosts of his ancestors, not in a place where the gods still laughed and said *not so fast*. They waited for the storm to pass and when it did, eventually, they climbed up and out and into the time after Rosamund.

Acknowledgments

This book would not have been made possible without help from the Arts Council of England, the Royal Literary Fund and the Author's Foundation, all of whom helped with funding which bought me time to write. *The Mermaid of Black Conch* was born from a number of sources: Neruda's famous poem "The Fable of the Mermaid and the Drunks", a strange true story of an event after a fishing competition in Charlotteville, Tobago, in 2013, the finding of the story of Aycayia, and countless dreams and even nightmares of a mermaid being pulled from the sea. The catch scene owes partial homage to Hemingway's *Islands in the Stream*. Also thanks to Anthony Joseph, whose advice I listened to early on, and who pointed me to "The Handsomest Drowned Man in the World" by Gabriel García Márquez. Myths of mermaids, sirens, exist in every part of the world, often young women cursed by other women. This story re-imagines an attempt to reintegrate an ancient exiled woman into modern life in the Caribbean. Thanks to Hannah Bannister and Jeremy Poynting at Peepal Tree Press for publishing the first edition of this book. Thanks to Alex Russell, at Vintage, for taking it onwards and to my editor at Knopf, John Freeman, for this U.S. edition. Piero Guerrini and Yvette Roffey, again, thanks for a place

Acknowledgments

to write. Thank you to Isobel Dixon, my agent of many years, for her belief in this mermaid. Isobel was instrumental in dragging this legend from the sea. A special thank-you and gesture of humble gratitude, too, for the womxn I know and admire, and who have helped carry my spirits this far: Karen Martinez, Lucy Hannah, Alake Pilgrim, Hadassah Williams, Gilberte O'Sullivan, Ira Mathur, Lisa Allen Agostini, Sonja Dumas, Anna Levi, Shivanee Ramlochan, Jannine Horsford, Jacqueline Bishop and Loretta Collins Klobah. Sistren of the pen, all.

A NOTE ABOUT THE AUTHOR

Monique Roffey was born in Port of Spain, Trinidad. She is the author of six novels and a memoir. *The Mermaid of Black Conch* won the Costa Book of the Year and the Costa Novel Award 2020, was shortlisted for the Rathbones Folio Prize 2021 and the Goldsmiths Prize 2020, and is longlisted for the Orwell Prize for Political Fiction 2021 and the OCM Bocas Prize for Caribbean Literature 2021. Her highly acclaimed previous books are *sun dog*, *The White Woman on the Green Bicycle* (shortlisted for the Orange Prize for Fiction 2010), *Archipelago* (winner of the OCM Bocas Prize for Caribbean Literature 2013), *House of Ashes* (shortlisted for the Costa Novel Award 2014), *The Tryst* and *With the Kisses of His Mouth*. Monique Roffey is a senior lecturer at the Manchester Writing School at Manchester Metropolitan University and a tutor for the National Writers Centre. She lives in the East End of London.

A NOTE ON THE TYPE

The text of this book was set in Requiem, a typeface designed by Jonathan Hoefler (born 1970) and released in the late 1990s by the Hoefler Type Foundry. It was derived from a set of inscriptional capitals appearing in Ludovico Vicentino degli Arrighi's 1523 writing manual, *Il Modo di Temperare le Penne*. A master scribe, Arrighi is remembered as an exemplar of the chancery italic, a style revived in Requiem Italic.

Composed by North Market Street Graphics,
Lancaster, Pennsylvania

Printed and bound by Berryville Graphics,
Berryville, Virginia

Designed by Betty Lew